Diana Best is an award-winning writer and journalist who spent most of her teenage years reading magazines during science lessons and flirting with boys. Her work in magazines often involves interviewing boys, bands and the Prime Minister at Downing Street, but thankfully not all at the same time. She lives in London with her husband Dan and their two cats.

Diana Best

bliss Life coach

Lads and Love

Everything you need
to know about
boys and you!

Piccadilly Press • London

*For my mum, who got me where I am;
my husband, who's the best boy in the
world; and my mates, who are the most fabulous
and wonderful people I could ever wish to know. I owe
you all chocolate.*

First published in Great Britain in 2007
by Piccadilly Press Ltd,
5 Castle Road, London NW1 8PR

A catalogue record for this book is available
from the British Library

ISBN: 978 1 85340 921 9 (trade paperback)

1 3 5 7 9 10 8 6 4 2

Printed in the UK by CPI Bookmarque, Croydon, CR0 4TD
Text design by Fiona Webb
Cover design by Simon Davis

Contents

Introduction

'Why do lads act so immature?'
'Why won't he call me his girlfriend?'
'Does boob size really matter?'

These are the kind of things we're asked every day at *bliss* – and this book provides the answers to those questions and more!

Boys can seem totally confusing and relationships can be a bit of a minefield. There's flirting to tackle, dating obstacles to navigate and the whole going-out palaver to baffle you. But it needn't be so difficult. With our expert advice, tips and inside information, you can learn to be a lad-expert and boost your relationship know-how – instantly! And there are loads of action plans and exercises to make sure you put it into practice. So let's get started!

CHAPTER 1

'God, he's sooo fit'

It started off as a perfectly normal day. Your alarm clock went off four times and only stopped when you chucked it at the floor. Your hair wouldn't go flat, you couldn't find your favourite skirt (the one that makes you look like Christina Aguilera) and were halfway down the road before you realised you'd left your mobile on the kitchen counter. But as you come rushing through the school gates, you stop dead. Leaning against the wall in front of you is the most gorgeous lad you've ever clapped eyes on – he's new, he's in your class and all you can do is giggle, blush and just hope he realises you're made for each other.

But sadly, lads don't have the in-built radar we all wish they did – one that enables him to pick up on your 'Hellooo, I fancy you!' vibes at a hundred paces. And believe it or not, lads can be really shy and a bit intimidated by us girls. So instead of waiting around, hoping he'll appreciate the extra lip-gloss you put on this morning, here's how to bag him before anyone else gets their sticky paws on him . . .

Grab his attention (the blush-free way)

Sure, micro-skirts and a push-up bra will have his eyes out on stalks, but we're talking about getting and KEEPING his attention here. It's true boys tend to go for looks more than girls do, but that's only a fraction of the package they're looking for.

Boys fall for the same things girls do: they like a girl they can relax with and chat to, someone intelligent and funny that they share interests with. Hoisting your boobs up round your neck with a bit of underwire is as likely to put him off as it is to hook him in.

✪ **If you want to catch his eye, blending in with the crowd just isn't an option.** This is where your unique individuality really works for you. Got gorgeous long hair? Wear it loose. Great smile? Flash it. Always been told you've got fabulous elbows? Show them off. Absolutely everyone has something uniquely beautiful about them – figure out what yours is, and use it!

✪ **Rope in your mates.** Hang out with them when your crush is around and have a laugh. Tell jokes that make everyone listen to you, even if they're daft ones your dad told you. The idea is to look chatty and friendly, not so mardy you'd sink a ship with your mood. It might be easier if you actually tell your mates what you're up to – they'll be in a better position to make you look good if they know who you've got your eye on.

✪ **Once you think he's looking, break away from your mates now and then.** A big gaggle of shrieking girls can put the fear of God into any lad who's trying to approach you. Make it a bit easy for him and go to the loo on your own, walking past him slowly on the way!

✪ **Ditch the attitude.** Pretending to be a bitch doesn't impress anyone and just makes you look mean and unapproachable.

'I remember when I first clapped eyes on Pete. He was in the Year above, and everyone really fancied him. I was a bit cheeky actually – I winked at him from across the cafeteria! But it worked.'

Lizzy, 17, Tunbridge Wells

3

YOUR ACTION PLAN:

✪ My unique selling point is:............................

....

✪ I'm going to show it off by:..........................

....

✪ The mates I'm going to enlist to help me get
   his attention are:.......................................

....

Fail-safe flirting tips

Unless you've got tomato stuck in your teeth, if
he's staring at you, he's interested. But you can bet
he's also thinking, 'If I ask her out and she says
no, that's it – I'm never leaving the house again!'

So, he stares at you in the hope he'll pick up a
clue that you like him. Lads don't need much
encouragement if they're keen – saying hi when
you pass him in the corridor might just be enough.

Whether he finally wanders over to you, or you
take the plunge and chat to him first, there are
some can't-fail flirting rules that'll make the whole
thing much, much easier.

Smile!
A big beaming face is way more attractive than a sour, grumpy one.

Chin up
Hold your head up and your shoulders back at all times. Confidence is incredibly sexy – and even if you don't feel it, this way you'll always look it.

Eye eye
Look him in the eye. We're not talking about a staring contest, though – remember to blink!

Be open
Don't cross your arms or put your hands in your pockets – this body language screams 'Get away from me!' Instead, use your hand to tuck your hair behind your ear now and then, or briefly touch him on the arm (go on, be brave!). It'll make him subconsciously think you're a warm person that he'd like to get to know better.

DO IT NOW! The key to sorting your flirting style is to practise. When you're at home and unlikely to be disturbed, stand in front of a mirror and practise the moves above. Yeah, you might feel daft at first, but it'll help you see what works best for you, and make you feel more relaxed when it comes to doing it for real.

Does he really fancy me?

Lads are great at expressing their emotion . . . when Rooney's just scored a winning goal. But when it comes to telling us girls how they feel, they can be totally crap.

So will you ever find out if Max in your chemistry class is actually trying to tell you something over the Bunsen burner? Yes – so stop wondering now! Lads are sending you flirt signals all time; you just need to know how to read them. Check out his body language and find out here whether Max fancies you – or if he's just got a particularly nasty itch . . .

The Peacock
When a peacock wants a date, he shows off his fancy feathers. If a lad looks at you while running his fingers through his hair, he's either rehearsing for a Head & Shoulders ad or he *really* likes what he sees.

The Bodybuilder
Back straight, tummy in, chest out. These moves are normally associated with us girls, but they're also busted by the loved-up lad. Subconsciously, he wants to make his chest look bigger and show he's strong enough to take care of you. Bless!

The Cowboy
It's no secret that lads are obsessed by their bits.
By standing with his legs apart and hands on hips,
this lad subconsciously wants you to think he's, er,
manly. The Cowboy is competitive, especially if he
spies another lad chatting you up.

The Helter-skelter
If a really cute lad's chatting to your best mate,
but his body and feet are turned towards you,
don't worry – it's YOU he really wants to get to
know. He's just plucking up the courage!

The Tortoise
If a naturally-shy lad's nervous about talking
to a girl he fancies, he tucks his head into his
shoulders to make himself invisible. Smile sweetly
to bring him out of his shell.

The Worshipper
A lad might shower you with compliments, but is
he *really* being sincere? If he says you look great
and shows you the palms of his hands, he
definitely thinks you're hot stuff!

DO IT NOW! Look him in the eyes when you chat to
him, then drop your gaze to his lips – then look
back at his eyes. Do this subtly a few times and
he'll feel a strong desire to kiss you!

Five telling little flirt signals:

- ✪ **Eyebrow flash:** If a lad's into you, he'll raise his eyebrows when he first sees you.
- ✪ **Million-dollar smile:** True smile will give him wrinkles around the eyes; fake ones don't.
- ✪ **Forward thinking:** When a lad's dazzled by your conversation, he'll lean in closer, with his chest and shoulders facing you.
- ✪ **Mirror, mirror:** If a lad likes you, he'll copy your body language without even realising it, so keep an eye on his gestures.
- ✪ **Toe-tale signs:** To suss his feelings, just look at his toes. His foot will point towards the most interesting thing in the room – hopefully you!

It's time to move on if . . .

1. His foot's aimed at the door. This shows he wants to escape!

2. His hands are in his pockets. This means he's in no mood for a chat.

3. He gives you a tight-lipped smile. He's being polite but he sees you as more mate than date.

FACT: It takes us just 90 seconds to decide if we fancy someone.

FACT: 55% of our opinion is based on their body language.

Revealed! How to pull absolutely any lad

It would be easy to lump all lads together in a big box labelled *Totally Confusing*, but don't give up so easily! If you can figure out his boy-type before you go in for the kill, it is possible to bag any lad. Just as you wouldn't wear the same outfit to both a party and an interview, you need to adapt your pulling style depending on the kind of lad you're after. So whether you're after a skater, townie, emo or geek, there's one rule to successful pulling: wow him with a little insider knowledge . . .

The Skater
Where you'll find him: Startling old ladies in the shopping centre or anywhere with lots of railings and concrete.
He'll rate you if: You can master an Ollie jump (check out www.skateboarding.com to find out how). It's simple, but shows you're serious – and you can ask him to help you master some trickier moves.
Chat him up with: 'Nice Vans! Has anyone told you you look like Tony Hawk?'

The Emo

Where you'll find him: In the queue outside downtown gig venues or with his headphones on in the park.

He'll rate you if: You tell him you've got tickets to a hot upcoming gig.

Chat him up with: 'Great hair! What do you use to get it to stand up like that?'

The Townie

Where you'll find him: Kicking back at JD Sports or at the bus stop, admiring his brilliant white Reeboks.

He'll rate you if: You're wearing more designer logos than his all-time hip-hop hero. It's all about the labels . . .

Chat him up with: 'I'm totally loving your Burberry cap. Where'd you get it from?'

The Geek

Where you'll find him: In the games section of HMV or checking out the *Star Wars* dolls at Forbidden Planet.

He'll rate you if: You beat him at his favourite online fantasy game. You are a warrior queen!

Chat him up with: 'I can't believe my dad didn't realise *Torchwood* is an anagram of *Doctor Who*. Who's your favourite character?'

'I have a thing for scruffy rock kids, and Dan ticked all the boxes. He worked in a record shop so I swotted up on the latest bands, then went in pretending to look for a rare promo album. One hour later, I had his number.'

Mel, 16, Plymouth

Chat up lines: The Good, The Bad and The Ugly

Chat-up lines are the knock-knock jokes of flirting. By and large, we'd never really recommend them as the route to a lad's heart – they're cringey, fake, and make you sound totally unoriginal. Having said that, here are a few we just had to share . . .

The Good
'I seem to have lost my phone number. Can I have yours?'

The Bad
'I tattooed this barcode on my arm so you could check me out.'

The Ugly
'Did you fart? Because you just blew me away!'

All unlikely to bag you a date, but good if you fancy making your mates crack up!

Five better ways to make an impression

Don't come across like a total try-hard, have a go
with these instead:

Say hello
There's nothing wrong with being friendly.

Get him involved in your conversation
Ask him to settle a discussion you're having with
your mate – it's an easy way to get him chatting.

Help him relax
Does he look a bit uncomfortable? Unless you're
wearing a *My ex-boyfriend's an axe-murderer*
T-shirt, chances are he's just shy. Get him to relax
by asking him something easy, such as 'I like your
T-shirt – where'd you get it?'

Ask him stuff
Ask him loads of questions about himself. Anyone
is flattered by people showing an interest in them.

Listen and nod
Listen to the answers and nod now and then. Even if
you've no idea what he's talking about, he'll be convinced you have a deep and meaningful connection!

DO IT NOW! Plan what you're going to say as your opening line and write it here:

....

....

....

....

....

'I always sat next to Ian in Biology – he was really funny and we'd have a right laugh together. After a few months, I realised I was beginning to seriously fancy him. I was too shy to say anything to his face, so I slipped a note inside his textbook at the end of class one day telling him how amazing I thought he was and how he made me feel. But the next day at school, everyone kept making weird smooching noises at me and asking when Ian and I were going to get married. Turned out he'd lent his textbook to the school loudmouth that night, who'd found it and blabbed to everyone! Even now Ian goes bright pink if I go near him.'

Jodie, 14, Winnersh

FACT: The first things most guys notice about a girl are her eyes and her smile. Draw attention to your eyes by tilting your chin down very slightly when you're looking at him – this will make your eyes look bigger and more appealing. Plus, a wide, happy smile is a killer smile!

Your ultimate pull sorted: because no one's out of your league

Justin Timberlake, your older bro's mate, or that hot lad you've had your eye on for ages – it doesn't matter who the lad you fancy is, chances are you've put him on a pedestal and are convinced he's never going to look your way.

But don't give up just yet, because getting him is much easier than you might think. A lot of it comes down to your own self-belief. If you give off the right vibe when you're around the lad you fancy, he'll find himself mysteriously drawn to you.

So before you settle for second best and decide it's less hassle to go out with a minger, follow these tactics and you'll soon be celebrating your first month anniversary with the boy of your dreams!

When he's older . . .

Landing an older lad is a piece of cake. It's all
about how you act in front of him. So keep your
passion for watching Disney flicks in your pyjamas
hidden and use your body language to get noticed.
And avoid nervous fidgeting or hair flicking,
because an older lad will see this as cheesy
flirting. Instead, plaster a huge smile on your face
and think Keira Knightley gliding down the red
carpet. Elegance equals maturity.

When he's gorgeous . . .

Hard to believe, but boys don't *just* go for looks.
What's more, confidence is beauty, so fake it.
Picture the most confident person you know, and
copy their body language. Also, attractive people
are more touchy-feely because they're more
comfortable with themselves, so try lightly
touching him on the elbow for two seconds when
you're chatting to get him thinking about you in a
girlfriend way. But be warned: he may be fit, but
your little toe could have more personality.

When he's cooler . . .

OK, so he wanders around in sunglasses and
designer jeans and makes your heart beat faster
just by looking in your direction. But is he
really all that? Being cool is about having the

confidence to know who you are and what you like, and about not being afraid to show it. It doesn't matter if you're into one thing and he's into something totally different – what matters is having an opinion. So when you're talking to him, don't feel like you have to agree with everything he says. If you disagree, hold your head up and explain why. Cool boys like girls who stand up for themselves and don't follow the crowd.

REMIND YOURSELF

Repeat the following at least once a day: 'No one is out of my league.' It's true! There are no such things as 'leagues' and you're perfectly capable of pulling any lad you like.

'There's this idea at my college that I'm this ultra-cool guy, I guess because I'm in a band and go to a lot of parties. So the girls who come up to me are always the loud, posey types. But the truth is I prefer girls who are much more quiet. Anything else just seems fake.'

Michael, 17, Holyhead

*'Everyone at school knows Jared – he acts
in his spare time on TV soaps, and is
unbelievably hot. The trouble is, he knows it.
Jared's used to girls fawning all over him, so
I went out of my way to ignore him – at
school, in the park, at the bus stop. Sure
enough, it worked! I guess I stood out; he
chatted me up one day and we ended up
dating for four months.'*

Angi, 15, Twickenham

Just a month to make him yours

You know that bloke who's making your heart do
somersaults? *Still* staring at him from afar? Well,
it's time to do something about it! This diary can
help you find out if he's the perfect lad or a
perfect loser. Each week, monitor his behaviour
and fill in the chart. If you're not happy with the
way your crush is progressing, try the tasks to
kick-start the romance. If he keeps passing your
tests, he'll be yours by the end of the month –
guaranteed!

WEEK ONE

I've got my eye on _____

My action plan!

Tick all the statements that apply to you this week:

O You doodle his name.
O You know his email address – and you've used it.
O He smiles and touches his hair when he speaks to you.
O He keeps looking at you.

Ticked two or more? Go to week two.
Ticked fewer? Try these tips then start the week again!

Tips of the week

To get his attention: When you see him, make sure to catch his eye and flash him a smile.

To make him yours: Catch his eye, hold his gaze for three seconds, *then* smile.

Jerk alert: If you spot him looking at your boobs for more than three seconds, steer clear!

NOTES:
If you get stuck at week one (and you've tried all the tips), it's time to find a new lad!

WEEK TWO

My action plan!

Tick all the statements that apply to you this week:

O He's been asking your mates where you are.
O He sends you a text at least once a day.
O He brushes against you.

Ticked two or more? Go to week three.
Ticked fewer? Try these tips then start this week again!

Tips of the week

To get his attention: When you're chatting, pay him a compliment.

To make him yours: Follow up the compliment with a question. Heard him play guitar? Ask him if he's in a band.

Jerk alert: Ditch him if he keeps banging on about how gorgeous your best mate is.

NOTES:
Going off your bloke? Restart this diary with any lad every time you fancy someone new.

WEEK THREE

My action plan!

Tick all the statements that apply to you this week:

○ You walk to the bus stop with him.
○ He burns you a CD or MP3.
○ Your mate's told him you fancy him – and he keeps coming over for a chat.

Ticked two or more? Go to week four.
Ticked fewer? Try these tips then start this week again!

Tips of the week

To get his attention: Subtly brush past him, or make some sort of physical contact.

To make him yours: Touch his arm or brush your leg against his. While you're making contact, 'spontaneously' ask him a question.

Jerk alert: Heard he's a serial snogger who boasts about his sexploits? Crush over.

NOTES:
You don't have to rush into anything – your crush can last more than four weeks if you like!

WEEK FOUR

My action plan!

Tick all the statements that apply to you this week:

O He keeps finding reasons to touch you.
O He asks you out.
O At a party, he singles you out for a dance or chat.

Ticked two or more? He's all yours!
Ticked fewer? Try these tips then start this week again!

Tips of the week

To get his attention: Organise a big night out, and make sure he's invited.

To make him yours: When you're talking to him, keep glancing at his lips – it'll make him long to snog you.

Jerk alert: If he's always late to meet you without good reason, get rid of the loser!

Crush closure: Now he should be gagging to ask you out, so get him alone at an opportune moment (like in the garden at a mate's party) and he'll grab the chance to make his move. If he doesn't, why not take the plunge and ask him out yourself? If you've got this far, the chances are he'll say yes.

Your weekend pulling timetable

Don't have a month? Need faster results? Transform your love life in 72 hours and get a snog by Sunday.

FRIDAY

Morning: It's time to make contact with your crush. Ask his advice, like how to turn on Blue-tooth on your mobile. He'll feel appreciated and manly, and you'll have something to talk about.

Midday: Back up this morning's ice-breaker by asking him for change in the canteen queue – then ask what he's up to after school. Name drop one of his mates – he'll feel like you're already in his circle.

Afternoon: If he told you he does after-school band practice or sport, head to the music block or playing field. Use his name when you talk to him – it'll make him feel important. Don't leave without getting his email address.

Evening: Get online and arrange for a small group to meet in town tomorrow – him included. Go on to his Myspace to find out about stuff he's into. You can ask him about them when you meet up . . .

SATURDAY

Morning: Pick an outfit that's sexy but casual –
loads of cleavage hanging out will just look tarty.
When you meet up with him and your mates,
send flirt signals by catching his eye for two
seconds, smiling, then looking away.

Midday: All this flirt work should be making you
hungry, so suggest a lunch stop-off at Maccy D's.
Ask if you can nick one of his chips; if he offers
happily, he's well into you. If he does it less
happily, you need to flirt harder!

Afternoon: Instead of running straight for the
nearest shoe shop, break away from your mates
for twenty minutes to wander round his favourite
shops with him and ask the questions you
prepared last night – he'll be flattered that you're
interested in him. Remember to ask him what
films he's into. . .

Evening: Lads like girls who are independent and
do their own thing, so head off for a girls' night
out without him. Play it cool and don't send so
much as a text. You never know, he might end up
texting you.

SUNDAY

Morning: Check out the cinema listings and – be brave – send him a text asking if he fancies seeing a movie with you tonight. Make it lighthearted but tempting: text *'Fancy grabbing a pizza then catching a movie tonight? x'*

Midday: Suggest to one of his mates that you all meet up for a game of footie in the park – and get him to make sure your crush comes too. But leave the baggy grey joggers at home!

Afternoon: Throw yourself into the spirit of the match and have fun! Enthusiasm is really appealing, even if you're the world's worst goal-scorer – and it shows you're not some princess who's scared of breaking a nail.

Evening: Watching a film in a dark cinema together is a perfect time to get closer. Bury your face in his arm if it's a grisly bit, grip his knee if you're scared, or give him a squeeze if there's a happy ending. The kiss will come naturally!

FACT: 90% of guys would love a girl to ask them out. But 90% of girls think a guy should do the asking!

Dealing with PPPs (Potential Pulling Pitfalls)

The path to your dream pull is rarely straightforward, but read this and you'll be prepared for anything.

Oh no! What if he doesn't fancy me?

For a start, just as we don't all fancy the same guys, guys don't all fancy the same girls. But there are so many reasons he might not want to go out with you – he could have a girlfriend already, he could still be pining over his ex, he could be gay! Don't assume it's all about you, because often it's not.

Everyone has to deal with rejection at some point; it's just part of life. But it's better to find out than to spend the next five years thinking *'I wish I'd asked that guy out – I wonder what he'd have said!'*

If you're feeling down, here are five simple steps for an instant mood-boost:

Step one: Go to your room, get your pillow, and scream into it. Really, really loudly. Maybe do it when no one else is home, so you don't freak out your parents.

Step two: Find three songs that make you happy and make you want to jump up and down. Put them on and dance like an *X Factor* reject for ten minutes.

Step three: Get your mates round, put loads of face masks and make-up on each other, read some mags and watch a DVD or two. Go on, be a total girl.

Step four: Write a list of ten things that are brilliant about you. Yup, the fact you've got amazing teeth, that you're a great listener, the way you can spot a must-have bargain at fifty paces . . .

1...

2...

3...

4...

5...

6...

7...

8...

9...

10...

Step five: Come up with your ultimate top ten famous boys you'd love to go out with. Thinking about it will remind you there are so many fitter, sexier lads out there to drool over.

1...

2...

3...

4...

5...

6...

7...

8...

9...

10...

Give it a month and you'll be sooo over it.

Aargh! What to do when a lad you don't fancy asks you out

This is a flattering situation to be in, but always a bit awkward. It takes a lot of courage to ask someone out, and he deserves to be let down gently, preferably not in front of other people.

It's best to be direct so there's no confusion. Tell him: 'I'm really flattered you asked, but I'm sorry, I don't want to go out with you.' If he asks why, just explain that you think he's a great guy, but you just don't fancy him. You might feel bad at the time, but you'll be relieved you were honest afterwards.

When the lad you're secretly drooling over is your best mate

When you spend loads of time with a guy friend, have tons of fun together and think he's great, it makes sense that you might start to feel a strong attraction towards him. The line between being friends with a boy and wanting to go out with him is often a pretty fine one.

THE 'DOES HE FANCY ME?' CHECKLIST

O Does he text you when he's in bed?
O Does he lend you his coat or jumper when it's cold?
O Does he ever put his arm around you, give you hugs or playful tickles?
O Does he choose to spend more time with you than his boy mates?
O Does he talk to you about other girls he fancies – but it turns out they're never anything serious?

If you ticked yes to all five, chances are high that he does fancy you. But think hard before you decide to say anything, because your friendship could be jeopardised if he doesn't feel the same way and he might end up feeling awkward around you. If you think you'll explode/start crying on him if you have to hold it in any longer, here's how to do it:

- ✪ It's best to explain your feelings when you're alone with him, rather than trying to jump him.
- ✪ Tell him you think he's a great friend, but that recently you've started to feel a bit more for him.
- ✪ Now, watch for his reaction. If he looks like he wants to hear more, you could either ask him straight out how he feels, or be slightly more subtle and suggest the two of you go out sometime on a . . . you know . . . DATE.
- ✪ If he starts to back off, tell him you really don't want to ruin your friendship and you want to give him time to think about it.
- ✪ Ask him to call you in a couple of days. That way he doesn't feel pressured to answer straight away, and once the surprise has worn off he may realise he feels the same way.
- ✪ If he hasn't called after a week, you may have to accept he doesn't feel the same way. Send

him an email explaining that your friendship means a lot to you and you're sorry if you've made him feel awkward.

✪ Even if he doesn't fancy you back, he'll appreciate that you gave him the space to think about what you said – and you'll have a better chance of being able to stay mates. You'll need to act normally around him to put him at ease, which isn't easy. But you'll find that in time it gets better.

✪ On the more positive side, you may find he flings his arms around you and declares his undying love. The thing is, you won't know unless you ask!

Lad confidence: tricks and tips

This might sounds cheesy, but it totally works. Remind yourself every day that you deserve an amazing lad. Before you chat to a guy you fancy, repeat in your head, 'Any guy would be lucky to have me!' This positive thinking seriously affects how you hold yourself and how other people respond to you – do it for a month and you'll see the results.

Try making up your own mantra. Imagine what would be the greatest compliment someone could give you, and write it below:

....

....

....

....

This is your secret confidence weapon. Repeat it to your self five times a day, and it will come true!

Know what you like, and you'll get it

Make a list of all the guys you fancy (famous and non-famous) here. Write next to each lad what it is you like about him, from his floppy hair to his love of punk music to the cute way he eats his lunch:

NAME   **WHAT I LOVE ABOUT HIM**

• ....

• ....

• ....

- ....
- ....
- ....
- ....

When you've finished, look over your list. Are there certain characteristics or traits that keep popping up? Do you go for guys who are sweet and intelligent, or guys who are a bit dangerous and rugged? Are you won over by athletic types, or do you go for the grungy indie kid every time? The more aware you are of your 'type', the easier it becomes to work out what you really want from a lad, and what things you're willing to compromise on.

Burning questions: you ask, we answer

Q. *I see this lad on the bus to school every day and I can't stop thinking about him. He's eighteen, but I'm only thirteen. Do you think he'll ever go out with me?*

A. Why is it that the one gorgeous lad you see all month turns out to be too old/ too weird/ gay?

It's just the way it happens sometimes. And when you're thirteen, a five-year age gap is just too big. When a lad is eighteen, he's at a completely different stage in his life to you, and your interests and tastes are likely to be totally different too. Plus, an eighteen-year-old might demand things emotionally and physically from a girlfriend that you're just not ready to give; remember, sex under the age of sixteen is illegal. He may be gorgeous, but he's just not worth it. We guarantee that within a few months you'll find someone closer to your own age who's much cuter anyway.

Q. *I've got a major crush on my teacher, but it's freaking me out – he's got a moustache and he's old enough to be my dad! Am I a freak?*

A. No, you're not a freak – it might feel weird to be lusting after a father figure instead of Orlando Bloom, but it's normal for girls to project their feelings onto someone older at some point. Boys your own age can seem really immature, and fancying someone out of reach is a safe way of experimenting with your feelings. Just make sure you keep your crush at a distance, and it'll pass in time.

Q. *I'm totally obsessed with Johnny Depp. My whole bedroom is covered in posters of him, I keep copies of every interview he's ever done, and I dream of flying out to meet him. Some days I cry so much – I worry we won't end up together. Is it normal to feel this way?*

A. What you're feeling is absolutely normal, but it sounds like your crush is getting a bit too painful for you to handle. We fancy famous guys because they seem so perfect – they're wonderfully romantic in movies, they always have great hair, and seem so much more mature than the boys around us. But that's just an image – if you spent any time with old Johnny you'd realise he farts, gets spots and is grumpy at times, just like the rest of us! So while it's fine to have a crush on him, try looking round at the lads you see every day. You might find that there's someone you could like a lot – and is better than a digitally enhanced 2D film star any day.

Q. *I think I'm quite pretty, and I've got lots of friends so I can't be completely awful. But for some reason guys never ask me out. Why don't lads fancy me?*

A. It sounds like lots of lads probably do fancy you – but are too afraid to tell you! For a lad, going up to a girl they fancy who's always surrounded by her mates is more daunting than doing a streak across a football pitch. If you see a guy you fancy, make it easier for him by saying hello now and then, and watch girls who are often talking to boys to see how they behave and interact. Remind yourself daily that you're pretty and popular: believing in yourself is incredibly attractive to lads. Be friendly and think positively and you'll find you get a lot more dates.

Q. *Every time a lad comes up to talk to me, I blush and stammer and make a total idiot of myself. How can I learn to just act normally around boys?*

A. It's easy to think of lads as these alien species that you need amazing powers to communicate with. But in many, many ways, boys are just like us girls! If a lad comes up to you, trust us – he'll be feeling twice as nervous as you, even if he doesn't show it. Remember, you're the one in control in these situations. He's not analysing your every facial twitch or blink, he's concentrating on not sounding like a moron. So take a deep breath in and out, push your shoulders down and hold your head up, and imagine you're chatting to an old lady at a bus stop. Yup, works like a dream.

Q. *Me and my mate both fancied the same guy for ages, and promised each other we'd never make a move. But when I came back from my hols, she confessed she snogged him at a party. I feel so betrayed and I never want to speak to her again.*

A. It's understandable that you feel let down by your friend, but the fact that she owned up to what she'd done shows she has some consideration for your feelings – she didn't let you find out from just anyone. You both kept your pact for a long time, so don't lose a good friend over a moment of weakness. At the end of the day, he's just a lad – there are plenty of them out there and you'll soon find another to drool over.

Q. *The other night my best mate came round to watch a scary movie. But when we snuggled up together under the duvet as usual, I suddenly had this weird urge to kiss her. Does that make me a lesbian?*

A. Everyone has a few moments in their life when they consider what it might be like to be intimate with someone of the same sex. The feeling can be especially strong around people we're close to, like our best mates. There's nothing wrong with feeling like this, but trying to make a move on your friend would be a bad idea unless you know she feels the same way. Your teenage years are your experimental

years, when you're working out who you are
and what you like, so for the moment, keep your
fantasy to yourself – if you enjoy just thinking
about it, you don't have to stop. If you feel it's
something more than that, talk to someone who
understands how you're feeling, like
www.gayyouthuk.org.uk (see the 'Further
Information' section at the back of this book).

It's a wrap!

By now you have:

- ⊘ Discovered how to catch his eye (the
  embarrassment-free way).
- ⊘ Boosted your boy-approaching confidence.
- ⊘ Learnt the most effective ways to flirt.
- ⊘ Sussed his flirt signals.
- ⊘ Figured out what you're really looking for in a
  boyfriend.
- ⊘ Learnt how to reel in any lad.

Going forward, make sure you:

- ✪ Know what your unique selling point is (and
  how to work it).
- ✪ Practise your flirt moves.
- ✪ Keep your confidence high with positive
  thinking.

CHAPTER 2

Dating SOS

Y ou've spied him, you've flirted your socks off, and you've bagged a date! But where do you go? How do you wow him and leave him begging for more? And how do you get out of it if you sent a *'Uurgh, he was horrible'* text to your date instead of your mate? Read on . . .

Where to head for first date success

Stumped for where to go? Take this quiz and it'll all become clear.

1. What's more important:
a) Getting to know each other
b) Getting a snog

2. Brr – you're feeling the chill! It's:
a) A chance to snuggle up
b) Time to put the heating on

3. You've got the house to yourself – do you:
a) Chuck on a DVD
b) Turn the stereo up – loud

4. Walking down the road you spot your bus pulling in at the stop. Do you:
a) Sprint like crazy to catch it
b) Decide you'll wait ten minutes for the next one

5. Being scared makes you:
a) Heart-pumpingly excited
b) Feel like crying

Now add up your points:

1. a) 2 points   b) 3 points
2. a) 3 points   b) 1 point
3. a) 2 points   b) 1 point
4. a) 1 point   b) 3 points
5. a) 1 point   b) 3 points

6-8 points
You're . . . a thrill seeker

9-11 points
You're . . . a heartfelt dater

12-14 points
You're . . . a romance lover

If you're a thrill seeker try:

Bowling
For: So daft it's guaranteed to make you laugh.
Against: Who's ever looked good in rented bowling shoes?

The funfair
For: You've got an excuse to grab hold of his arm on the ghost train.
Against: Throwing up on the rides – not a good look.

Ice-skating
For: The chance to look graceful as you swan about on the ice.
Against: The chance to fall on your bum so often you get frostbite.

If you're a heartfelt dater try:

Going for coffee
For: It doesn't cost much and you can get away early if it's not going well.
Against: If caffeine makes you jittery it's not great for first date nerves!

Heading to a gig
For: If you both love the band you'll have a great time.
Against: Watching Death Rock Hallelujah when you're not really into it isn't much fun.

Going for a game of pool
For: If you're good at it, it'll be fun; if you're rubbish at it, he can put his arms round you and show you how to play . . .
Against: Cues are long – beware of smacking him in the danglies with it.

If you're a romance lover try:

A walk round the park
For: Feeding the ducks together – cheap and romantic!
Against: If it's the middle of winter it'll be freeeeeezing.

Going for pizza
For: You can actually talk and hey – there's food, always a bonus!
Against: High potential for throwing tomato sauce down your new top.

The cinema
For: The excitement of waiting to see if he'll snog you in the dark.
Against: You can't chat and get to know each other without being shushed.

FACT: Most people believe dating becomes a relationship after two months.

Getting around strict parentals

It can be hard to remember, but at the end of the day your parents are only trying to look out for you. Bear this in mind and you'll have a better chance of persuading them you deserve a bit more freedom.

✪ Ask them to explain their reasons for not letting you go out. Worried about your homework? Make sure you do it in advance. Haven't met your new lad? Ask him to come in and say hi before you head out.

✪ Keep calm – if you start shouting or crying with frustration, it'll just make them believe you really are too young to be trusted. Point out that you can't earn their trust unless they give you the chance to earn it.

✪ Try to work with them a bit. If it helps, agree you'll only go on dates in the afternoon. When they realise nothing awful's going to happen they might loosen up a bit.

✪ Agree a reasonable time to get home – and stick to it. It might seem way too early to you, but something is better than nothing.

YOUR ACTION PLAN
To help you keep a clear head and plan what
you're going to say, write down your plan of action
and the main points you're going to make here:

1...

....

2...

....

3...

....

Who pays?

Always make sure you've got money to pay your
half on the date, and offer to pay your share. If he
insists on paying for you, say thank you and enjoy
it – don't spend ages arguing over it!

Boys aren't expected to pay for everything and
there's no reason they should other than good old-
fashioned tradition. Prove you're independent by
paying your way at least some of the time. Lads
don't like to feel like they're being taken for a ride.

How to guarantee
a second date

If you're on a date already, you can pretty much guarantee he's interested. The key to getting a second date now is to hold back a bit. So don't go telling him your entire dating history, your chronic wind problems and the fact you've got a huge crush on Simon Cowell. If you tell him everything there is to know about you in one go, there's nothing for him to find out next time – and you'll be so full-on you could scare him off!

✪ Try to ask as many questions as you answer – it'll help you have a conversation rather than make it seem like an interview.

✪ Be relaxed and chatty, but keep it lighthearted.

✪ By the end of the date he should feel like he's only just started getting to know you – but he wants to know more.

✪ If you fancy him, let him know! So many boys don't call again 'cos they've got the mistaken impression you're not interested. Smiling, looking him in the eye and touching him lightly on the arm when you're talking will subtly let him know you're keen.

✪ If you want to give him a kiss at the end of the date, go ahead – but don't let it go on too long. Like we said, the idea is to leave him desperate to see you again!

✪ End by saying, 'I had a really great time tonight – I hope we can do this again soon.'

'I was dying to snog Harry at the end of our first date, but I held off because I didn't have any chewing gum and I was worried he'd hate my pizza breath. It wasn't till we'd been dating for eight months that he told me my initial "shyness" was what made him fall for me.'
Adelaide, 14, Stoke-on-Trent

If you'd rather swim with sharks than see him again

If he tries to kiss you at the end of the date and the idea of it just makes your skin crawl, be firm. Smile politely, step out of the way, and say, *'Thanks for a great night. I'll call you.'*

Then send him a text the next day saying: *'I had a great time, but to be honest I don't see you as more than a friend. I hope we can be mates.'*

It's straightforward and makes your feelings really clear – go you!

The new text & email rules

Technology: it makes our lives so much easier and so much more complicated all at the same time. There you are, merrily texting your mate Jen about the awful date you had with 'Hairy Bob' last night, when – oops – you suddenly realise you did in fact send it to one Mr H Bob. And he's REALLY narked.

We've all been there – so how do you make sure you keep these gaffs to a minimum?

✪ If you're tempted to send a text when you're angry or upset, don't do it! Put the phone down, leave room and go and do something else while you calm down. You'll thank yourself for it . . .

✪ If you don't trust yourself not to ring that lad up and start crying/telling him you love him, give your phone to a friend for safekeeping.

✪ Delete numbers of people you shouldn't be calling from your phone, so you can't accidentally send them the wrong message or get in touch when you're feeling emotional.

✪ Read your message out loud before you send it – something that sounds funny in your head might sound plain rude when it's written down.

✪ Email is especially dodgy. How would you feel if someone forwarded your email on? If the thought makes you feel uncomfortable, tone your message down a bit.

✪ Think before you press send – is that the right address you're sending to? Have you clicked on 'reply all' by mistake? Are you even replying to the right person?

Great get-outs if you've slipped up

'My mate/mum/bro borrowed my phone 'cos they were out of credit.'

'Hel-*lo* – I was talking about [insert name of male celeb], of course!'

'Someone forwarded that to me as a joke – isn't it funny?'

'Oh, my mate/mum/bro was asking me something while I was typing and I got distracted.'

'What are you talking about, I didn't send that! Someone must know my email password . . .'

'Oh, my phone's been stolen!'

FACT: 27% of us have sent a text or email to the wrong person – and suffered the consequences. Oops!

DO IT NOW! Send a flirty text to that lad you fancy. If you need motivation, think of it this way – in just a few minutes you could have date with him all set up for this Friday night . . .

Cringe!

'I have officially the biggest-ever crush on my best mate's older brother Anthony, so when I was round her house one evening I quickly sneaked into his room to have a snoop about. When I spotted his bed, I couldn't resist jumping on it and giving his lovely soft pillow a good, long sniff – and that's when Anthony walked in and caught me! I just wanted to die. Now every time I go round my mate's house, he won't look me in the eye and leaves the room. Not quite the effect I wanted!'

Sarah, 15, Bootle

'I'd been waiting for months for Nick to ask me out, so when he finally asked me to the end of year disco I was beyond excited. At home I spent ages carefully applying concealer, put on coats of mascara for really fluttery lashes and slicked on a load of lip-gloss to finish. As I strutted through the

*flashing UV lights towards him in my miniskirt
and heels, I knew I looked the bomb – so I
was surprised when he looked at me strangely.
That's when his mate leaned over his shoulder
and went, "Hey, Emma – your spots are
glowing in the dark!" Aargh! I'll always blend
more carefully in future.'*

Emma, 14, Taunton

*'My older sis is at university and I grab every
chance I can to hang out with her and her
cool mates. Last summer she threw a party at
a pub in town and all her friends came down
for the weekend, but mum banned me from
going, saying I was too young. But that didn't
stop me! On the night, I crept out the back
door and legged it across the fields to join the
party. I was in the middle of chatting to this
drop-dead-gorgeous English undergraduate
when the door to the pub burst open. The
music stopped and everyone turned to stare as
Mum appeared in her pink fluffy slippers
yelling, "Rebecca, get in my car this instant!"
Mortified doesn't begin to cover it.'*

Becky, 16, Sidcup

10 steps to being a super-snogger

There are few things more exciting than leaning in to kiss someone you really fancy for the first time. It's thrilling – look who *I'm* pulling! And it's nerve-wracking – what if I get it wrong?

Everybody has their own way of kissing – but there are a few little changes you can make that'll turn you into a five star super-snogger.

Step one: Make eye contact. It's the only way you'll know for sure if he fancies a snog too – and it'll help you get the timing right.

Step two: Tilt your head a little to the side, so you don't bump noses!

Step three: Gently press your lips against his for a second or two. Remember to breathe through your nose.

Step four: Then open your mouth slightly, and touch the tip of your tongue to the tip of his tongue.

Step five: You can play with it a bit here – circle or lick his tongue with the tip of yours, explore a little, do whatever feels nice. Have fun with it!

Step six: Gently hold onto his shoulders or the back of his head if you want to.

Step seven: Some people like running the tip of their tongue briefly over the other person's lips.

Step eight: You can try sucking his bottom or top lip, very gently, for a second or two.

Step nine: Lads aren't just sensitive on their lips – his neck, ears and eyelids are all good places to gently touch your lips and get him tingling.

Step ten: Tease him by breaking away from the kiss early – you'll leave him wanting more.

DO IT NOW! Keep chewing gum and lip balm to hand so when the time comes, you're minty fresh and your lips are kissably soft! Boys prefer kissing baby-soft lips instead of lips covered in sticky gloss or lipstick.

FACT: 80% of people tip their head to the right when they go in for a snog.

Snogging explained: why it feels so great

Getting off with someone doesn't just make you feel like the world's most attractive person – it has tons of other benefits too. Research shows that couples who kiss a lot are more likely to be faithful to each other, so make sure you're planting plenty of smackers on him! It's also great for your figure, helping you burn an extra twenty-six calories a minute – must be because your heart's pumping so fast!

Passionate kissing also releases a hormone called oxytocine, with makes you feel more loving, and creates endorphins which give you a major adrenaline rush similar to hurtling along on a rollercoaster – but much, much sexier!

'My most memorable snog was on my ex-boyfriend's sofa last summer when we were babysitting his little brother. We were lying on the sofa together, getting quite heated, when water exploded over us. His brother had crept downstairs and thrown a water balloon at my head! You could say it cooled things down a bit.'

Kirsty, 16, Manchester

Your hot three questions answered

1. What's the right way to do it?

The answer is: on top of a washing machine on the fourth Friday of every month. No, not really – because there is no right way to do it. It's like crisps: everyone likes something different. Generally speaking, you might want to avoid biting, licking the other person's face, and moving your tongue frantically like it's on a spin cycle (unless you know the other person likes that). Kissing is about exploring, going with the flow and doing whatever feels right.

2. What if I do it wrong?

It isn't a test! No one does it right all the time. The key is to take it slowly and gently work out what you like.

3. What if I don't like it?

Bad snog? Don't worry, you're not a freak – it's just a matter of finding a kissing style you enjoy. Keep practising and you'll soon get the hang of it.

Boys reveal . . .
what makes a girl sexy

And it's not all boobs, bums and tongueing:

'Swinging her hips when she walks.'

Alex, 15, Leeds

'If she laughs and looks like she knows how to enjoy herself.'

Phil, 17, High Wyckham

'A bit of shyness is good – it draws you in.'

Elliott, 19, Newport

'Smiling, every time.'

Ben, 16, Macclesfield

'Showing off her arse!'

Rico, 16, London

'The way a girl looks at you, then looks away again – a real tease.'

Dave, 17, Newcastle

'She just needs to be herself, nothing fake.'

Peter, 15, Derby

'Dressing a bit unique always catches my eye and makes me think, "This girl's different".'

Jason, 18, Cheltenham

Meet the parents . . .

There's no doubt about it, meeting your lad's parents for the first time is a nerve-wracking experience. There are so many questions: Will they like me? Will I like them? What if they serve fish for dinner (I hate fish)?

If all's going well with your new lad, it's likely that you'll meet his folks at some point – and it needn't be a terrifying ordeal!

Bear a few things in mind:

✪ No matter what his parents are like, they managed to spawn the gorgeous being who is now your boyfriend. Be grateful!

✪ His parents will want to like you. They're not going to hope you're some crazy devil-worshipper. They'll be looking for the good things about you, not analysing your faults.

YOUR 'MAKE THEM LOVE YOU' ACTION PLAN

1) Bring them a present. A box of chocolates, some flowers, some embroidered teatowels from Cornwall that your mum doesn't want – the gesture will make you look thoughtful.

2) Offer to help with stuff like setting the table, but avoid offering to help with the roast if beans on toast is the limit of your cooking skills.

3) Be polite and smiley, and don't swear. It's not ladylike, and parents *love* ladylike.

4) Never slag off their son – not even jokingly. They might be able to laugh about how he's never been able to hold down a part-time job, but it's not OK for you to join in!

5) Instead, talk about how wonderful he is. You can be as gushing as you like here: parents will believe anything about their kids.

6) Laugh at his dad's jokes. It doesn't matter how old they are, boys love girls who think they've got a great sense of humour.

Basically, be an extra-polite version of your normal self and they'll love you! Then you can sit back and spend half an hour laughing at the baby pics of your lad that his mum brings out . . .

DO IT NOW! Make a list of five parent-impressing things you can tell your boyfriend's parents about yourself so you're ready to fill any awkward silences – from your great mock-GCSE grades to your brilliance at playing the guitar to how you help your mum clean the house every weekend:

1...

....

2...

....

3...

....

4...

....

5...

....

Reminding yourself of your achievements before you go will give you more confidence and help you relax!

Burning questions: you ask, we answer

Q. *I went out with a totally gorgeous guy and we had a great time. He said he'd call, but I've been waiting over two weeks now. Why hasn't he called?*

A. I hate to say it, but it sounds like he's just not that into you – and has taken the coward's way out of telling you. If a lad's keen he'll call you within a week of your first date. But past a week, he's either not really bothered or he's not going to call at all. There's always the chance he's lost his mobile or is in hospital with a broken leg, but to be honest it's not that likely – it's time to move on and find a better lad.

Q. *I've never kissed a guy, but all my mates have. I feel like a total weirdo – what's wrong with me?*

A. You might be feeling a bit left behind, but you're certainly not a freak! There's a lot to be said for taking your time with these things and not rushing into it. Your mates might have snogged lads before you, but who's to say it was a good experience? Maybe they wish they hadn't rushed into it. Wait for a guy you really like to come along, and things will happen naturally. You'll get your snog one day soon.

Q. *At a party last week I snogged a lad I have a major crush on, but now he's blanking me. What went wrong?*

A. Sounds like this guy finds you attractive, but isn't looking for a long-term relationship and doesn't know how to tell you. When you've drooled over someone for months, it's hard to accept a snog won't turn into something more. But if he's being childish enough to ignore you over it, do you really want to go out with him anyway?

It's a wrap!

By now you have:

- ⊘ Sussed your perfect date venue.
- ⊘ Sorted your parents.
- ⊘ Bagged a second date.
- ⊘ Figured out how to let someone down gracefully.
- ⊘ Learnt to be a snogging queen.
- ⊘ Won over his parents.

Going forward make sure you:

- ✪ Keep up any promises you've made to your parents.
- ✪ Remember the rules of guaranteeing a second date – they'll get you through the first five or six dates, too.
- ✪ Don't stress about snogging techniques – you'll be a pro before you know it!

CHAPTER 3

Lads decoded

L ighting farts, boasting about sex and winning the Foot Odour Of The Year award . . . if you've ever thought boys were a different species, you may be right! But underneath all that, lads are pretty straightforward creatures. Here we'll help you understand how they tick – and why.

First, list all those baffling things you just don't get about boys here:

.... ☐

.... ☐

.... ☐

.... ☐

.... ☐

By the end of this chapter you should have a much better understanding of what's going on in his head and bod! Tick off each one as you solve it.

We knew there was a reason for the Adam's apple

When a lad makes you wonder 'Why did he do that?' the answer may be simpler than you think. Much boy behaviour is explained by what happens to his body as he matures. When a boy hits puberty, his testicles start producing the male sex hormone, testosterone. This makes him grow body hair, develop muscles and gain an interest in – or rather an obsession with – sex! So in the name of science and for the sanity of all girls, here's a guide to what's going on. . .

Change of heart

One minute his lips are glued to yours, the next he acts like you don't exist. Why? To use a cliché, it's not you, it's him. In their mid-teens, lads fall in love (or lust) very quickly, but they're often not mature enough for long-term attachments. So, try not to take it personally. Just make sure he doesn't take you for a ride.

Mood swings

As much as we love 'em, lads can be a bit sulky. It's partly hormonal, but it's also their way of coping with their changing appearance. Lads do worry about their bodies, and shut themselves off when they feel insecure. If you're into him, a little flattery goes a long way!

The mind boggles

If he swears he 'forgot' to call you, in all likelihood he's telling the truth. The area of the brain responsible for planning and organisation develops more slowly for lads, so things tend to slip their minds!

Face facts

His growing facial fuzz is all thanks to a super-strong type of testosterone that only lads produce (phew!). Most boys are dead chuffed when they first grow bumfluff, so never diss his 'tache.

Finding his voice

Testosterone makes his voice box tilt, giving him an Adam's apple. Meanwhile, his vocal chords get thicker and longer, making his voice 'break'. When this happens, some lads' voices are squeaky one minute, booming the next. He may find this embarrassing. So, if he grunts rather than talks to you, you know why.

Booby prize

You might dislike being seen in a bikini, but lots

of lads also hate getting their chests out. It's because, like us, many boys get boobs (yes, boobs!) in their teens. They don't grow as big as ours, and they tend to disappear after puberty, but having boy-baps can make a lad feel very self-conscious.

Boy to beefcake
Ever wondered why a lad can scoff three Big Macs and not have a spare ounce of fat on him? It's thanks to the testosterone having a toning effect on his body and making him more buff. Not fair!

What's up?
When a lad hits puberty, his testicles (the dangly balls behind the penis) and penis grow larger and pubic hair starts to grow at the base of his willy. His testicles also begin to produce sperm and he'll start getting erections. At first, lads find erections hard to control. Add to this the fact that his hormones make him think about sex every six seconds, and you've got to kinda feel sorry for him!

Hanging low
So, why are lads such cry-babies when they get hit in the goolies? The testicles are one of the most sensitive parts of a lad's body, and even more so when he's going through puberty. It's because

the testicles 'drop' further away from his body (meaning there's no bone or muscle protecting them), making them extremely delicate!

Head over heels

If he trips over his feet when you're around, it's not just because you make him nervous. When boys get their growth spurt, their hands and feet grow faster than the rest of their body, making him a tad clumsy. Bless.

FACT: Both girls' and boys' bodies contain testosterone, but boys have ten times more!

DO IT NOW! We all have insecurities, but tend to focus on our own so much that we completely forget boys have them too. So, time to drop the baggage! Write your top five insecurities here:

1...

2...

3...

4...

5...

Now, take a deep breath and close your eyes. As you blow out heavily through your mouth, push your shoulders down and imagine you're blowing all your negative thoughts out of your body. Then, if your first insecurity is, 'I hate my bum', in your head shout 'I love my bum!' Do the same for all five. It works because physically blowing out your negative thoughts allows you to let positive ones in to replace them. Try it!

Why do lads . . .?

They're male, they're baffling, they talk about amplifiers and gears like they're actually interesting . . . so who better than some lads to explain some of their weirder behaviour?

Q. *Why're lads so crap at chatting on the phone?*

A. *'While girls use the phone to gossip, guys just see it as a means to an end. Have you ever heard a bloke on the phone to his mates? "Yup, uh-huh. . . OK, see you at five. Sweet." And that's it – no hello, no goodbye, just straight to the point. After all, why waste time on the phone if I'm going to see you in four hours? Frankly, if you're getting anything more than that out of a guy, you're doing* *really well because it means he's making an effort.'*

Daniel, 15, Solihull

Q. *Why won't he hold my hand in public?*

A. *'That's easy – he's embarrassed. Holding a girl's hand is a public statement of how you feel, and it's not that easy for us to make. I worry my mates will laugh. Plus I think it makes a girl seem possessive. At the end of the day though, if I like a girl enough, I'll do it.'*

Simon, 17, Reading

Q. *Why'd he rather play footie on Saturdays than spend time with me?*

A. *'Saturday afternoon football sessions are a really important bonding time for guys. It's easy to understand if you think about it – girls have shopping, guys have sports. It's like this big social event where guys can be all blokey and run around a lot. You wouldn't like it if we tried to stop you shopping, so leave us to our football. We'll thank you for it in the end!'*

Ed, 18, Norwich

YOUR ACTION PLAN:

List the things you want from him here – for example, 'I'd like him to meet my mates'. Read to the end of the chapter, then come back and fill in how you think you can achieve each one.

What I want from him:

1..

2..

3..

4..

5..

How I can get it:

1..

2..

3..

4..

5..

The lingo of love

What he says and what he really means

Lads – they just can't say what they really mean,
can they? Their fear of putting their foot in it
makes them come out with some really weird stuff
at times. Luckily, this handy guide will leave you in
doubt about what he's actually trying to say . . .

He says: It's not you, it's me.
He means: I just don't fancy you.

He says: I'm sorry, I just forgot to call you.
He means: I was playing Death Match 3 at
Jason's house.

He says: I'm just not very good at talking
about how I feel.
He means: Are you actually going to MAKE me
say 'I love you'?

He says: Why are you wearing that short skirt?
He means: What if a more attractive bloke chats
you up?

He says: I didn't realise it would upset you.
He means: I hoped you wouldn't notice I did that.

He says: I can't afford to take you out tonight.
He means: I spent all my cash on a new iPod.

He says: Of course I got you a present!
He means: Oh crap, I forgot it was your birthday.

He says: Do you fancy coming out with my mates?

He means: I really want to show you off to my friends!

He says: I'm not sure I can make it to your mate's birthday party.

He means: The idea of meeting all your mates all at once terrifies me.

He says: I'll call you sometime.

He means: But hopefully you'll have forgotten I exist before then.

He says: I just need a bit more space.

He means: Er, like A LOT more space – leave me alone.

He says: I wasn't checking her out!

He means: Of course I was checking her out, I'm a boy. But you're my girlfriend and I like you a lot, so don't worry about it.

He says: [nothing]

He means: That thing you just said was weird. I'm thinking very hard about how to respond. Help me!

He says: I'm sorry.

He means: I'm sorry, I mean it and don't make me say it fifteen times to prove a point.

YOUR ACTION PLAN:

Now you're more familiar with boy-language, use this space to help decipher your lad.

He often says:...

I thought he meant:..

Now I realise he means:..

....

He often says:...

I thought he meant:..

Now I realise he means:..

....

He often says:...

I thought he meant:..

Now I realise he means:..

....

He often says:...

I thought he meant:..

Now I realise he means:..

....

Winning words – how to speak Boy

OK, we're all on the same planet. But when it comes to conversation, boys might as well come from Mars, because they clearly don't understand us girls – or they usually get the wrong end of the stick at least.

It's simple, really: don't give too much away, or (if you have to) be clever in how you say it. Study this list of five clangers, and take real lads' advice – this is what they'd prefer to hear . . .

SCENARIO ONE

You want to say: *'I know we've only been seeing each other for two weeks, but I think I've fallen for you!'*

If you do, he hears: *'I'm crazy. I'm desperate. And if you try to back off, I'll kill all your family and friends.'*

What you should say instead: *'The two weeks we've had together have been really great.'* Mark, 17, from Frome explains, *'The word "falling" is definitely too much this early in a relationship.'*

SCENARIO TWO

You want to say: *'But I want to go out with you on Saturday – why do you need to see your mates?'*

If you do, he hears: *'Stop hanging out with your friends and spend MORE time with me.'*

What you should say instead: *'Your mates are great, but there's something I want the two of us to do together this Saturday.' 'This is much less threatening,'* says Chris, 17, from Beckenham.

SCENARIO THREE

You want to say: *'Where on earth were you last night – and why didn't you return my messages?'*

If you do, he hears: *'You have to tell me where you are every minute of every day, or I'll assume you're cheating on me.'*

What you should say instead: *'I called last night but you were out. Are you around for a chat tonight instead?' Rob, 16, from London says, 'Don't turn into a stalker – that's just scary.'*

SCENARIO FOUR

You want to say: *'My ex would never have forgotten to call/bought me that/said that.'*

If you do, he hears: *'My ex was fitter and better than you, and if he calls, I'm so there.'*

What you should say instead: Eric, 17, from Portsmouth, says, *'Don't say anything! I don't think exes should ever be mentioned – it's horrible to be compared.'*

SCENARIO FIVE

You want to say: *'Now we've snogged/held hands/gone on a date, are you my boyfriend?'*

If you do, he hears: *'I'm coming on strong because I've been having a think about baby names . . .'*

What you should say instead: *'Someone asked me if you were my boyfriend, but I didn't know what to say.'* Ricky, 17, from Leeds explains, *'If he likes you, it'll be totally fine.'*

YOUR ACTION PLAN

Write what you really want to say to him here:

....

....

....

Think about how it will sound to him. Now, using the examples above, re-write it here:

....

....

....

Cringe!

'When my older brother's gorgeous mates came round to watch the footie one Saturday I was so excited! I immediately rang my best mate Claire on the upstairs phone and told her to get over to my house straightaway to check out the "serious studmuffins on the sofa". But when I strolled down ten minutes later, ready to flirt, my bro and all his mates cracked up. Turns out he knew what I was up to and they'd all listened in to my call on the downstairs line! I wanted to die.'

Robhyn, 15, Llandudno

10 simple questions to have him sussed

So you know he's mad about Man U and his dad's called Keith, but do you really know what makes your lad tick? Throw these bizarre but brilliant questions at him for a sneaky insight into what's going on inside his head.

You ask: How many pairs of shoes do you have?

He answers:..

Vanity comes Adidas-shaped for lads. Mr Happy-go-lucky will have a few pairs under the bed, but if he has more than 10 pairs then he could be Mr Vain!

You ask: What's your favourite movie?

He answers:..

If he likes romantic flicks, it means he's shy and sensitive. Fans of action movies are predictable in a blokeish kind of way.

You ask: What does the colour red make you think of?

He answers:..

If he thinks of love and passion, he's sexy and romantic. But be warned – if he thinks of danger or anger, he's a moody pessimist.

You ask: Do you want to dance?

He answers:..

An easy way to tell if your lad's Mr Self-Confidence or Mr Self-Conscious!

You ask: Do you have a pet at home?

He answers:..

If not, get him down to Pets R Us! Research shows pet owners are more likely to be sociable, loving types.

You ask: Wanna go halves on a bag of chips?

He answers:..

If he's too mean to share, he's selfish, but lads who do share are easy-going.

You ask: What's your mum like?

He answers:..

'She's nice' = cool. 'She's a cow' = a bit worrying.
'All women should be like her' = leg it now!

You ask: Who did you last get angry with?

He answers:..

Family rows are normal, and nothing to worry
about. But if he loses his rag with random people
then he's impulsive, opinionated and has a fiery
temper.

You ask: What scares you?

He answers:..

If he's willing to lower his defences and admit he's
not always a hero, he's more likely to be honest
and open.

You ask: What's in your pockets?

He answers:..

Lads don't carry much, so this says a lot about
them. Fluff and chewing gum show he's Mr
Carefree, while an iPod tucked inside a protective
case shows he's cautious. Pics of his ex in his
wallet means he's so not over her – run!

Pass his secret tests

Ever wondered why it takes so long for a lad to say you're going out? Secretly, he's checking if you're right for him. Here's the lads' lowdown on how to pass his sneaky tests . . .

1. The mate test

Fart jokes, dead arms, taking the piss – all things lads love doing with their mates. And it's super-important to your new bloke that you accept/cope with/pretend to like his mates – warts, shouting, belches and all.

How to pass: If you can't beat 'em, join 'em. Lads fart around because they want a reaction, so the more you laugh along with him, the more relaxed he'll be.

Whatever you do, don't: Enter into a fart-off with his mates.

PASSED ☐

2. The leer test

You go to his room and the walls are plastered with posters of glamour models . . . in leather knickers! *'Your reaction says a lot about how laid-back you are,'* says Paul, 15, from Clapton.

How to pass: Most girls will react with jealousy, but remember, it's you he wants to go out with. If you accept you can both have pin-ups, he'll be impressed.

Whatever you do, don't: Deface Jordan with a giant marker pen.

PASSED ☐

3. The gossip test

Most girls can talk for England, but lads need to know they can trust you. *'One ex blabbed all my most intimate secrets to her mates,'* says Joe, 18, from Carlisle. *'So I was nervous about going out with Clare. I told her one thing to see if she'd pass it on, but she didn't – result!'*

How to pass: Don't tell your mates his secrets. Spilling to the whole class about all your snogs will send him running too.

Whatever you do, don't: Tell his mum what a great snogger he is.

PASSED ☐

4. The other girl test

Can you keep your jealousy in check? *'I liked Courtney, but when I was around other girls she turned into a madwoman,'* says Robert, 17, from Perth. *'I was always matey – I didn't flirt – so it was really cringey. She had to go.'*

How to pass: You have to trust him – it's as simple as that, because jealousy can destroy a relationship. Truth is, if he really is the one for you, he won't let you down.

Whatever you do, don't: Bitch about his girl mates.

PASSED ☐

5. The clingy test

If there's one thing blokes can't handle, it's a girl who starts weeping the minute he does something without her.

How to pass: People need space, and it makes the time you have together so much more special. Make plans that don't always involve him. Being independent is attractive and strengthens relationships.

Whatever you do, don't: Buy matching outfits as a symbol of your everlasting love. Or get tattoos of his name.

PASSED ☐

FOR BONUS POINTS:
Offer to come and see his favourite football team play their next match. He'll love that you're making the effort!

'I knew Josh's mates meant everything to him, and getting in with them would be the key to winning him over. So I made an effort to hang out and chat about typical boy stuff – obscure bands, cars, West Ham FC. I was talking absolute rubbish and they knew it, but they thought I was really funny. Result!'

Julia, 18, Loughton

The insider secrets lads don't want you to know

Three things he won't change for you:
1. Absentmindedly rearranging his bits when he thinks you're not looking. Hey, it's relaxing.
2. Enjoying Girls Aloud music videos – on mute.
3. Checking out other girls – secretly.

Three texts he wishes you'd send:
1. *That's OK, u go watch footie with ur m8s*
2. *Yes, u really r the best snog I've eva had!*
3. *I'm on my way over – and I'm wearing THAT little skirt . . .*

Five signs he could be a stalker:
1. He calls more than three times a day, just to check up on you.
2. He comes over to your house and hangs out with your mum – even if you're not home.
3. He loses it if you don't answer your phone straight away.
4. He's suspicious of every guy you talk to – even your oldest mates.
5. He's really clingy and complains that you never pay him enough attention.

Five signs he's obsessed with his ex:
1. He still has a photo of her in his wallet.
2. He keeps calling you by his ex's name.
3. He can't stop bringing her up in conversation, despite the fact she doesn't have anything to do with what he's talking about. It shows he's still thinking about her.
4. He keeps all the stuff that she left over at his house.
5. He goes all quiet when 'their' song comes on the radio.

Three things you do that drive him wild:
1. Anything that involves touching your hair.
2. Stretching out then crossing your legs.
3. Eating a decent meal in front of him – and enjoying it!

Five signs you can't compete with his mum:
1. She irons his pants.
2. He talks about her all the time.
3. He calls to give her an update, halfway through your date.
4. She still makes him a packed lunch every day.
5. He accidentally calls you 'Mum'!

Three clues he's a control freak:
1. He butts in and corrects the 'facts' when you're telling a story.
2. He wants you to wear exactly what he likes, and sulks if you don't.
3. He loses it if you don't stick to his plans.

Four signs he likes you a lot:
1. He's happy when you succeed at something.
2. He forgives you when you're a narky cow.
3. He tries really hard to get on with your family.
4. He gives you his last caramel HobNob.

Four of his secret stresses:
1. Spots. At least girls can use concealer.
2. Being just as clueless as girls about dating.
3. Being too weedy.
4. That you fancy his best mate more than him.

'My really pricey moisturiser kept running out really fast – I couldn't understand it, and it was costing me loads. That's when my boyfriend Nick confessed he'd been sneakily swiping some whenever he came round – he said it made his skin soft. And he'd been using my tweezers on his nose hairs, too!'

Eileen, 17, Fife

DO IT NOW! If you really want your lad to open up to you, try listening to him. Because girls are naturally more talkative, we don't actively listen to lads as much as we could. So give him your undivided attention for half an hour. Let him talk about whatever he wants, just ask the odd question and listen. You'll be surprised what you find out!

It's a wrap!

By now you have:

- ⊘ Figured out why he acts the way he does.
- ⊘ Understood his insecurities and blitzed your own.
- ⊘ Worked out the difference between what he says and what he really means.
- ⊘ Learnt to communicate better.
- ⊘ Got him to do stuff that you want!

Going forward make sure you:

- ✪ Use your insider knowledge to relate to him better.
- ✪ Keep working on your insecurities – and remember you're not alone!

CHAPTER 4

You, him and everything in-between

Y ou might be at the oh-so-freaky 'My parents say do you want to come round for tea?' stage, or only be at 'Wow, that's a weird surname'. Either way, the whole going-out-together business can seem trickier than picking out the right pair of jeans at Topshop (and with as many potential disasters).

Going out with someone should be a rollercoaster of fun, not a massive chore. Working through this chapter will answer all your relationship questions and solve all your boyfriend dilemmas, leaving you free to relax and enjoy the ride!

10 things every great relationship needs

You've deciphered his lad-code, now here's a heads-up on how to move things forward. There are some special ingredients every good relationship needs if it's going to last.

1. Trust

This is really important. None of that constant 'Where are you now?' 'Why didn't you call?' business, or manically texting him all evening when he goes out with the lads. If you're with him, you have to believe in him until he gives you good reason not to. So instead of worrying, bury your mobile under a cushion and head round a mate's house for a good gossip and a bar of Fruit and Nut.

2. Understanding

Realise that if he's grumpy, it might not be about you; and if you need space, you need to know he'll give it to you. Relationships have ups and downs – allowing for that will give you a head start.

3. Stuff in common

So he likes watching Arsenal, and you like watching the latest hot singer on MTV. It's good to have separate interests to chat about, but also

CHAPTER 4: You, him and everything in-between

having stuff in common helps you bond – without it, you won't 'get' each other. Hey, he can pick up some dance moves with a bit of effort . . .!

4. Support
Being able to help each other through tough stuff like exams and parental probs is as important as being able to make each other laugh.

5. Respect
Parents and rappers are always banging on about respect. Here it means thinking about the other person and considering how they might feel about stuff, or even just leaving him the last Double Indulgence Chocolate Cookie when you know he loves them more than Arsenal.

6. Fun
When you're not busy understanding each other and being considerate, you've got to have a laugh together – from watching your favourite episode of *Little Britain* to catching him trying to cut his toenails with a pair of eyelash curlers.

7. Sharing stuff
Swapping thoughts about the latest Johnny Depp movie, opinions on his new maths teacher, splitting large vegetarian stuffed-crust pizzas, anything!

8. Effort

People who think good relationships are easy have got it wrong. After six months you should be more relaxed with each other than on your first date, but you should still consider how the other person feels and make an effort to make them happy.

9. Honesty

This doesn't mean admitting you've always fancied his older brother! But if you're lying to each other a lot or hiding something big, it'll only turn into a huge problem of Wembley-sized proportions later.

10. Love

It probably won't be there from the moment you clap eyes on each other (that's lust), but you'll need it at some point (see p.97).

FUTURE-PROOF YOUR RELATIONSHIP!

All this stuff is hugely important, but making sure you've got them all covered is hard. If you're in a relationship, have a big think about it and write down three things from the list above that you reckon you really need to work on:

1..

2..

3..

Now ask yourself how you can improve on these each day. For example, if you reckon you need to make more effort with each other, have a good think about what he's really into and plan a day out together around it. Once you've identified the areas that need work, it's much easier to think of ways to fix them.

> 'A good relationship means you have to stick up for each other.'
>
> Debbie, 14, London

'Did I tell you about the time I . . .?'

Getting to know a lad really well is one of the best things about having a boyfriend. Nothing beats the feeling that you can trust someone to keep your secrets, and having them trust you enough to do the same.

But watch out – 'cause there's some stuff you might want to think twice about telling him. It's fine to let your guard down and show him the sides of you that aren't 'perfect', but you can take it too far.

Stuff to share and stuff
to keep schtum about:

Share: that you once thought you'd marry Sawyer from *Lost*.
Don't share: that you still kiss his poster every night.

Share: that you wear make-up and don't get up in the morning looking 'perfect'.
Don't share: that you also love biting your toe-nails while watching *Friends*.

Share: those pics of you peeing on a golf course when you were two.
Don't share: those pics of you peeing on a golf course last year.

Share: your hopes of being a famous pop star one day.
Don't share: that you reckon he's got the singing voice of David Beckham on helium.

Share: your fear of spiders, rats and baked beans (hey, everyone has their thing).
Don't share: your fear he might one day dump you and run off with Lindsay Lohan, thereby leaving you broken-hearted and unable to watch *Mean Girls* ever again (it ain't gonna happen).

Telling him stuff that's hurtful isn't usually a good idea; sometimes, keeping your opinions to yourself is for the best. If you really hate something like his haircut and just have to tell him, do it tactfully. Saying, 'You really remind me of Orlando Bloom – his haircut would really suit you, y'know!' is a good way. Blurting out 'God, you really look like Shrek from this angle' is not.

DO IT NOW! Have a girls' night in with your mates, dig out loads of old pictures and laugh at all the stuff you used to get up. Some things are best shared with your mates!

Cringe!

'Adam and I had only been dating a month when his parents threw a massive party for their twentieth wedding anniversary. They're pretty well-off and it was a really impressive event, with a huge marquee in the garden and a jazz band. I was quite excited and had bought an amazing new dress, but on the day I woke up feeling a bit funny. Determined to make a good impression I threw myself into the party anyway and was doing OK, until Adam dragged me onto the dancefloor and suddenly twirled me around. Instantly I felt really sick – and promptly threw up spectacularly, all

*over his trousers and shoes. Needless to say
his family looked horrified, but Adam was
great and tried to convince me no one had
noticed. He took me home, but not before I
caught sight of his mum frantically mopping
at the puddle of sick with a pained expression
on her face. Nooooo!'*

Abbie, 17, Purley

Arguments

There's an idea that's been peddled by romantic
Hollywood movies and big ballad music videos
which says couples who're really in love never
argue. Of course this is totally crazy – how else
are you meant to work out whether to watch
X Factor or *Big Brother*? But seriously, we're all fed
the idea that real relationships are perfect and
true love means not having to make an effort.
This is a load of rubbish.

A good relationship means caring about the other
person enough to work through problems rather
than walking away from them. People who care
about each other don't force the other person to
agree with them, or make them do stuff they
don't want to.

And this is where arguments come in. Think of every argument you have as a step toward working out your differences. Every argument you get through brings you that bit closer to understanding each other (something else those Hollywood movies make look way too easy – we'll say it once: boys are not mind readers).

There are a couple of big, blinging golden rules when it comes to arguments:

- ✪ Disagreements need to be resolved, or they just eat away at your relationship and make you angry and resentful.
- ✪ Don't sink to the level of calling each other names. Yelling 'You're a wanker!' at him isn't going to help anything.

On a serious note, there are some lads who get so angry they lash out. This is something you should never, ever put up with. Violence is totally unacceptable and is a massive dealbreaker (see chapter 7). If someone's lashed out once, no matter how sorry they are, they'll probably do it again.

Work out your problems

Girls are a lot more emotional than lads – we think more often with our hearts than our heads. By taking time to reasonably work through your side of an argument, you've got a much better chance of sorting the whole thing out so . . .

✪ Think carefully about what it is that's upset or annoyed you. Was it the way he said something, or a certain word he used?

✪ Now look at how that made you feel. Often, we're not simply upset – maybe something he said made you scared he doesn't like you anymore? Perhaps you're worried about him, or think that something he did was out of order? Try to explain precisely what's bugging you.

✪ Think about what would make you happier about the situation. Is it a reasonable thing to ask? How would you feel if he asked that of you?

✪ Now tell him precisely what made you upset, and how it made you feel. It is really hard to do this, but it's worth it. Telling him, 'When you do that it makes me feel like this . . .' can help him understand where you're coming from.

✪ Ask what he thinks about what you've said. He should listen to what you have to say, and then you can suggest how you'd like to resolve things. He's way more likely to respond positively to this than crying or screaming!

How to tell if it's the real thing

Blimey, describing what love is is tricky. When you first meet a guy you like, you feel excitement, like having butterflies in your stomach – and that's a mixture of nerves and lust. But after a while, that feeling changes. You still feel excited to see him, but it's mixed with the feeling of liking that person just as they are. That's love.

But what about being 'in love'? Well, the general consensus is that there's a really funny feeling in your chest and stomach that happens when you're 'in love'. It's a different feeling to just loving someone – love comes from the heart. Being 'in love' is an encompassing, warm sensation that you get whenever you think of him. It's having a real, deep connection with someone.

Love might hit you almost instantly, or it might take months to grow. So don't get hung up on labelling what you feel. Enjoy being with your lad, and when it's love you'll know.

Those Three Little Words – saying 'I love you'

Being the first person to say 'I love you' takes a ton of courage, and you've got to be prepared for the fact that he might not feel the same way, or perhaps isn't ready to say it. But if you want to tell him, go for it – at the very least you'll know you were honest. Perhaps he's been dying to say it for ages too, but is too chicken!

Whatever you do though, pick your time carefully. Don't blurt it out when he's watching the World Cup or playing Death Raider 3 – chances are he won't be listening. And don't declare your undying love for the first time in front of his mates – he might be glad you've said it, but typical 'Oh my God, what will my mates think?' laddishness could stop him reacting the way he'd really like to.

The secret signs he's really into you

Lads are generally a bit crap when it comes to chatting about their feelings. While girls can dissect every last vowel in a lad's voicemail message, boys sit with their mates in front of *Soccer AM* with only the occasional 'Boot it Rooney!' between them.

That's not to say lads don't like talking about their feelings. They just find it a bit harder because a) there's still an idea that 'real lads don't get emotional', and b) boys take the piss out of other boys. It's difficult to bare your deepest emotions to your mates when Tony ends up shouting, 'Ooh, James has gone all soft on us!'

Being used to keeping emotions in means it can take a while for lads to open up to girls, so don't feel disappointed if he doesn't make the grand 'I love you' statement straight away. Lads give off little secret signs when they're really into you - and we've got the inside scoop on what they are.

Put a tick next to each example your lad does, then add them up at the end to see where you stand. And shh, don't tell him we told you!

○ He brings you stuff without you asking. A cup of tea, a Krispy Kreme donut, a CD by your favourite band . . . It's the little things that show he cares.

○ He makes sure you get home safely after you've been out – whether he walks you to your door, or puts you on the right bus and makes you promise to text when you get home.

○ He listens to you when you're talking (at least most of the time – boys are only human, like us).

○ He doesn't blab everything to his mates about intimate stuff you've got up to together. If he really likes you, he won't want the whole world to know all the details.

○ He's happy to be seen out with you, and is warm and smiley towards you in public. Lads in love aren't able to hide it.

○ He talks about you – to his mates, his mum, the milkman . . . He'll be so proud of you he won't be able to shut up.

○ He turns you into a football supporter. He's only going to spend time and energy getting you into his fave footie team if he knows he's going to be with you a while.

○ He thinks the way you sneeze like a baby gorilla is cute, when everyone else thinks it sounds like a squadron of fighter jets landing on the lawn.

○ He'll watch *Titanic* with you for the sixth time with only a minimal amount of complaining.

○ He'll make an effort to give you his opinion on your outfit when you ask. If he agrees on a trip to Topshop with you, you're onto a winner!

Now add your ticks up . . .

If you have 1-3 ticks
Hmm, he's not really making much effort, is he? This lad's too busy thinking about himself to show you the consideration you deserve. Remember, any lad should be happy to be seen with you and proud when he talks about you.

If you have 4-7 ticks
This lad's keen and clearly cares about you 'cause he's really started to look out for you. But there's still a lot of work to be done here. Any decent lad should accept you for who you are and make compromises to keep you happy sometimes.

If you have 8-10 ticks
Wow! Here's a lad so head over heels he'll do anything for you. You're a lucky lady 'cos he's showing real devotion. Bear in mind that this should be a two-way thing though – if he's putting in all this effort, make sure you're giving it back too.

'I knew he loved me when he remembered to get me one of those praline Flake bars instead of the boring plain one.'

Suze, 15, Cambridge

'He gave his feelings away when he let me share his dinner without complaining!'

Alice, 17, Sheffield

Decipher his lad strops

Boys like to believe that girls are the stroppy ones, prone to getting huffy at the slightest thing. But the truth is that lads do it too! Recognising when a lad strop is coming and learning how to respond to it can make your relationship much stronger. So, whether he's a screamer or a sulker, take this test and follow the resulting rules. The next time he throws a wobbly, you'll have him behaving like the best boyfriend in the world in no time!

Tick the statements that sound most like your lad when he's got a mood on . . .

Last week you had a row . . . he's still missing your calls 'by mistake'. ◯

He's stormed out of the cinema in a shower of popcorn because he reckoned you were leaning too close to the boy on the other side of you. ☐

102

Dewy eyes, wobbling lower lip – that's his usual look when he doesn't get everything his own way. △

OK, so strong silent types are incredibly sexy, but you're beginning to wonder if your lad's gone completely mute. That silence is doing your nut in! ◯

The last time you had a row, he smashed up his room, kicked some furniture and swore quite a lot. ☐

It's always you who ends up offering *him* a tissue, even though it's him who started the stupid row. △

Only his mates can get sense out of him when he's in a mood – he refuses to tell you what's wrong. ◯

People stop and stare when you're in the middle of a row because he's putting on such a dramatic firework show. ☐

It seems like every time you row, he plays the victim – making you feel guilty for disagreeing with him. △

If you ticked . . .

Mostly circles: **He's a sulker**
Instead of saying he's upset, he sulks and waits for you to notice. Then, when you ask what's wrong, he says, 'You should know,' and huffs off.

How to handle him: Don't pander to him. He needs to learn to communicate like a mature human being, so leave him to it until he does.

Mostly squares: **He's a floor-beater**
When something sets him off, he wants to whole world to know he's annoyed. He gets lairy and aggressive, like a bit of a psycho.

How to handle him: The worst thing you can do is lose your temper too. Leave the room – he'll soon calm down without an audience.

Mostly triangles: **He's a hurt pup**
He'll pout, make you out to be the baddie and bring out sob stories that have nothing to do with your row, just so you feel sorry for him.

How to handle him: You still have the right to air your views. Just wait until he's finished whining, or he won't be listening properly.

Get a life!

The most attractive girls aren't the ones who're the spitting image of Paris Hilton – they're the ones who clearly have busy lives to be getting on with. Lads love a chase, and hate girls who are clingy as they come across as desperate. When your life doesn't revolve around your lad, he'll feel flattered as it seems like you chose to be with him – not the other way round.

So don't hang around the phone waiting for him to call - head out to meet your mates. He can always leave a message (that's what voicemail was invented for). You'll have more to talk about when you do hook up and won't feel like you're suffocating each other!

It's also really important to keep up your friendships. You'd hate your mate to ditch you for a lad, so don't do it to her – and if things don't work out with your bloke you'll really need your good friends around you for post break-up pizzas and bitching!

Have you got the lads/mates/life balance right? To find out, keep a diary of what you do for one week and use it to fill in this chart:

Monday
Hours spent with friends: __ On schoolwork: __
With family: __ With your lad: __ On 'me' time: __

Tuesday
Hours spent with friends: __ On schoolwork: __
With family: __ With your lad: __ On 'me' time: __

Wednesday
Hours spent with friends: __ On schoolwork: __
With family: __ With your lad: __ On 'me' time: __

Thursday
Hours spent with friends: __ On schoolwork: __
With family: __ With your lad: __ On 'me' time: __

Friday
Hours spent with friends: __ On schoolwork: __
With family: __ With your lad: __ On 'me' time: __

Saturday
Hours spent with friends: __ On schoolwork: __
With family: __ With your lad: __ On 'me' time: __

Sunday
Hours spent with friends: __ On schoolwork: __
With family: __ With your lad: __ On 'me' time: __

TOTAL
Hours spent with friends: __ On schoolwork: __
With family: __ With your lad: __ On 'me' time: __

How balanced is your chart? Are you surprised to find you're spending way more time with your boyfriend than you though you were? Are your family and friends missing out on some quality time with you? Or are you just so busy you haven't got any 'me' time – time to crash on the sofa with a bag of Minstrels and a copy of *bliss*? The exercise opposite should help you see where you need to make changes in your life.

Boyfriends are great – but here are seven things girl mates can't be beaten on (so don't forget 'em)

1. **Girls' nights in:** Nail polishing, Ben and Jerry's Phish Food, and a DVD of *Bring It On*. Perfect.

2. **Emotional support:** When you tell a lad a problem, he has an inbuilt need to fix it. But often, we ladies just want someone to moan to. Girls are great at lending a sympathetic ear and murmuring, 'Poor you', or shouting 'The bastard!' at all the right points. Plus they don't freak out when you cry.

3. **Lending you embarrassing CDs:** Let's face it, he's unlikely to have that Chico album you secretly love.

4. **Giving an opinion:** You ask a lad how you look in that dress. He goes pink, mutters 'It's fine' and runs off. Ask a girl, and she'll tell you if it makes you look like Peter Kaye and if not, she'll pick out the perfect shoes to go with it.

5. **Being your entourage:** Girl mates are ready-made personal PRs, poised to stick up for you, big you up or boost your morale at any given time.

6. **Advice:** Your mates will often have been through similar stuff and will have read tons of agony aunt pages in women's mags, so are well-equipped to deal with most problems.

7. **Understanding the pain of waxing:** Lads will never get it.

List five things you can plan to do with your girlfriends over the next three months – and stick to it:

1..

2..

3..

4..

5..

Burning questions: you ask, we answer

Q. *My boyfriend hates it when I go out with my mates. He calls them slappers and reckons we should be spending more time together. But I love my mates! What should I do?*

A. Sounds like your lad is a tad on the possessive side. You need to keep an eye on this, 'cause it can get out of hand. Decent boyfriends know the importance of having your own mates and interests, and will trust you won't get up to anything behind their backs. Talk to him about his worries, and reassure him you have your own mind and can't be led astray, no matter what your mates are like. And think about arranging to see each other a couple of nights a week, when just the two of you can hang out and have fun.

Q. *Whenever I see my lad talking to another girl, I see red. I don't see why he has to talk to them when he's already got a girlfriend. Am I being unreasonable?*

A. There's a bit of the green-eyed monster at work here. Being jealous of other girls shows you're feeling a bit insecure about something – so think about what's *really* bothering you. Your lad should be able to talk to whoever he wants, and your behaviour is more likely to push him away than bring him closer. Loosen up, and remember all the reasons he's going out with YOU – and not them.

Q. *My boyfriend and I have been together for two and a half years, but now he's moving away to uni. It's the other side of the country and I won't be able to visit often. My mates think we'll split up, but I'm terrified at the thought of losing him. Are they right?*

A. Long-distance relationships are really hard to keep going, but it's not impossible. You've got a couple of years of shared memories to bond you across the miles, along with the phone, email, letters, texts and MSN! If you both make the effort to keep in touch you have a fighting chance. Schedule in a date for you to visit soon (one is better than none) so you've got something to look forward to, and take up some dance classes or something to keep you busy in the meantime.

Q. *I met a gorgeous lad on holiday last month. We hung out together all day, and kissed on the beach – it was so romantic. We swapped numbers* *and promised to keep in touch, but now I'm home and he's not answering his phone. What went wrong?*

A. The thing about holiday romances is that all that intense heat and the exotic surroundings send us a bit doolally. It feels like something straight out of a movie, and your romantic interest seems unbelievably perfect. Then you get back to regular old Basildon, real life takes over and the bubble bursts with a bang. Maybe this lad has a girlfriend; maybe he's not really that into you. But you just have to accept he's now avoiding you. Hang on to your fantastic holiday memories and remember he's really not as perfect as you thought he was – and you can do better.

It's a wrap!

By now you have:

⊘ Identified which bits of your relationship need work.

⊘ Learnt when to share and when to keep schtum.

⊘ Discovered how to effectively deal with any arguments.

⊘ Figured out if it's the real thing.

⊘ Worked out your boyfriend/life balance.

Going forward make sure you:

✪ Keep putting effort into your relationship.

✪ Try to stay calm when you disagree.

✪ Make time for things in your life other than your boyfriend.

CHAPTER 5

Doing 'it'

Sex seems to be everywhere – in films, on posters and popping up embarrassingly on prime-time TV shows you're watching with your parents. Knowing the facts – and your own mind – will help you work out what's best for you.

How do you know if you're ready?

Movies and TV shows may make it seem like sex isn't a big deal, but in reality there a lots of things you need to consider before you decide to have sex with someone, especially for the first time.

Girls find it more difficult than boys to separate sex from emotions, so you can end up feeling more vulnerable once you've done it. If you're not totally sure about your lad before you have sex and feel nervous or frightened, you might feel even worse afterwards – especially if you don't know him very well.

Having sex *does* change things, and not always for the better. You can only lose your virginity once – and you can't get it back afterwards, so think about it carefully.

Your 'Am I ready?' checklist:

Am I aged sixteen or over?
✪ Sex under the age of sixteen is illegal for both you and your partner.

Do *I* really want to do this, now? Or would I be happier waiting a bit?
✪ Having sex isn't something you want to rush – if you wait until you are totally prepared, it'll be much, much better.

Do I like and trust my lad? Do I wholeheartedly believe he respects me?
✪ If you feel you don't know him that well or are concerned about what he wants from you, wait!

Have I talked to him about sex, discussed how we both feel about it, and agreed on what contraception to use?
✪ All these things need to be discussed and agreed on in advance. If just talking about sex makes you laugh, you're not ready.

Am I clued-up about the risks involved, from sexually transmitted infections to pregnancy?

✪ Make sure you read the relevant sections in this chapter so you know what you're getting into.

Do I feel under pressure to have sex, from my lad or from friends?

✪ Don't believe everything your mates tell you. Teenagers are competitive; half of the people who say they've had sex haven't, and half of the ones who have had sex really didn't enjoy it because they rushed into it.

✪ If your lad has ever tried to convince you to have sex by saying, 'But everyone's doing it', 'You would if you loved me', or 'This will make our relationship stronger' – stop! Someone who tries to persuade you with emotional blackmail isn't putting your feelings first.

Does my gut instinct tell me that the time is right, and that this is a step I'm ready and willing to take?

✪ If you listen carefully, a small voice inside your head and heart is telling you the truth about how you feel and what you truly believe you should do. Can't hear the voice? Then you've got too many worries on your mind – you'd better wait a while longer.

If you have any doubts at all, don't do it. There's nothing wrong with waiting. Try talking about your concerns with a trusted friend or family member – someone you know only wants the best for you. Talking to a parent about sex can seem nerve-wracking, but most parents would rather you talked to them about it than kept your worries to yourself, and parents can give pretty great advice. After all, they know you well!

ACTION PLAN

Use this space to write down the things that are important to you and you need to discuss before you have sex. Seeing things in black and white will make matters clearer in your head and help you work out if he really is the right one.

....

....

....

....

....

....

FACT: The average age girls in the UK lose their virginity is seventeen.

CHAPTER 5: Doing 'it'

Saying no (and meaning it)

Repeat after us: 'No, I don't want to have sex'. Yup, it's that simple. You should NEVER do something you aren't comfortable with.

It can be hard to stick to your guns when someone you fancy or even love is putting pressure on you to give in. But your prerogative to say no is important, and you shouldn't forget that 'No' is a perfectly acceptable answer.

- ✪ You don't need to have reasons, and you don't have to explain yourself to anyone. A simple 'I don't want to' is fine.
- ✪ If you're talking to someone you care about and you want them to understand, talk to them calmly and list your reasons. 'I'm not ready', 'I don't know you well enough' and 'I'm waiting for the right person' are all valid answers.
- ✪ If they aren't listening to you, don't carry on kissing. If they keep trying to change your mind, push them away and say 'No' again.
- ✪ If you feel uncomfortable, it's best to leave and talk about it when you're both feeling calmer.

YOUR MANTRA: 'I don't have to do anything I don't want to do.'

Keep saying it until you really mean it.

'I decided when I was thirteen that I wanted to save sex till I got married, because I want to make it really special. I told my last boyfriend after a few weeks, but I don't think he took me seriously. He kept jokily trying to get me into bed. After the first couple of times it wasn't funny any more. I realised he wasn't the kind of guy to wait, and ended it. Weirdly, we're really good mates now!'

Stacey, 17, Belfast

Is he after love or just sex? How to sort the playas from the stayas

So, you're finally seeing that hot lad and he seems keen on you. But does he want you as a girlfriend, or is he really just after sex?

Boys can give off mixed signals that are hard to read, but there are ways to tell if he's genuine. Tick the statements that apply to your boy, count up what shape you have most of and read your results . . .

When you're in a group, he:

Asks your opinion ○

Blatantly checks out other girls □

Listens to your opinion △

Finds excuses to brush against you ○

Spends most of the time trying to get you alone □

Is always chatting with you △

Acts like a joker ○

Makes dirty remarks about you □

Is impossible to get away from his mates ○

When it's just you and him, he:

Looks in your eyes a lot △

Doesn't suggest going out to do stuff together □

Is not keen on getting physical with you ○

When you kiss, he:

Doesn't always try to move things on △

Goes a bit quiet ○

Sulks if you move away from wandering hands ☐

When he's on the phone, he:

Goes on about how all of his mates are
having sex ☐

Confesses he's fancied you for a very long time △

Is mute and blatantly watching *EastEnders* ☐

Asks when you're free and organises dates △

Mostly chats about music and stuff on telly ○

Accidentally calls you by another girl's name ☐

Laughs at your jokes and asks after
your mum △

Hangs up first ○

If you ticked mostly squares: **He's a playa**
Sorry, but this boy just wants to get you into bed.
If you snogged him and he never called again,
could you handle it? If you're not sure, you must
talk to him. You may hear something you don't
like, but better now than later.

If you ticked mostly circles: **He's an either-waya**
Jokey one minute, trying to suck your face off the
next? He's unsure of what he wants! Boys mess
around because they're terrified of showing their
feelings. Get him away from his mates – then see
how he acts. Chances are he'll be sweet and not
at all pushy.

If you ticked mostly triangles: **He's a staya**
He respects you and he's after more than just
a quick fumble. But what if *you* want to get
physical? Boys can be shy about sex too, so try
talking about your relationship and how he feels
about sex. And remember, it's illegal to have sex
unless you're both over sixteen.

Boys answer your hot topic: 'Would you dump a girl if she said no to sex?'

'Never – that's not what having a girlfriend is about.'

James, 17, Greenock

'No – what loser would?'

Finn, 16, York

'No way – I've been in that situation myself!'

Marlon, 18, Thurso

WRITE IT HERE! Think carefully about the things *you* need to feel totally happy and comfortable with before you have sex, and jot them here. Use this page to remind yourself of your needs and standards, and hold off until you've fulfilled all of them:

....

....

....

....

....

Sex myths busted

'You've got to have sex with me or my balls will burst!' It's a classic male mid-snog plea, and one that would send most girls diving for the exit. But sadly there are a lot of lads out there willing to tell lies to get a shag, and a lot of people who've got their facts about sex *really* mixed up. So here's a selection of the planet's greatest sex nonsense, put straight.

If a bloke doesn't have sex regularly his testicles will explode

Complete and utter, er, balls. If a bloke's turned-on and doesn't ejaculate (come), the most he's likely to feel is a mild ache down below. Aroused girls experience the same sensation, and sex isn't the only way to deal with it. He can masturbate until he comes, or leave it and the feeling will go away. Some lads think unless they ejaculate, their balls will fill up and burst. In fact, unused sperm is just broken down and absorbed back into their bodies.

You can't get pregnant unless a boy ejaculates inside you

Sorry ladies, but you really can. Boys can produce a liquid from the tip of the penis as soon as

they're even slightly turned on. It's called
pre-come and is full of baby-making sperm. Even
if a lad's penis isn't inside you, any sperm that
gets into your vagina will head for your eggs.
So to avoid an unwanted pregnancy and nasty
sexually transmitted infections (STIs), put a
condom on him as soon as he gets an erection.
You can find out more about STIs later in this
chapter.

HIV is mainly contracted by gay men

False! Anyone can contract an STI or HIV, and
over half of the people who contract HIV in the
UK each year are straight. And cases of chlamydia
(which can lead to infertility if left untreated) in
teens are skyrocketing. To protect yourself, always
use a condom and get regular check-ups at your
local sexual health clinic.

If you only have oral sex, anal sex or lesbian sex, you're still a virgin

This is a difficult one. The technical definition of
losing your virginity means the penis has to enter
the vagina, but in reality it means different things
to different people. One thing is for sure: you can
get an STI from all these types of sex. So don't get
hung up on labels; just make sure what you're
doing is safe.

As long as you're on the Pill, and have a long-term boyfriend, you don't have to use condoms

False. Using the Pill properly will stop you getting pregnant, but only condoms protect against STIs (see 'Contraception' below). Loads of people have STIs and don't know it because they don't show any symptoms. Using condoms as well as the Pill stops you from worrying something's about to go horribly wrong.

You can tell if someone has an STI

Face facts: you can't. Anyone can get an STI, and you can't tell if someone has one just by looking at them. So always play it safe and use a condom.

You can't get pregnant the first time you have sex/if you do it on your period/if you do it standing up

Sex was designed to make babies, and if jumping, bathing and standing on your head were reliable forms of contraception, humans would have died out pretty fast. Not only are sperm very determined, but they can survive in your body for up to seven days – so even if you're on your period, they're in with a fighting chance of being fertilised.

Girls don't masturbate

Rubbish – a lot of girls bring themselves to orgasm, they just don't talk about it as much as boys do.

Despite this, it's a totally normal part of female life, and a really enjoyable way to explore your body. That means that when you do eventually decide to have sex, you'll know what feels good and can point your lad in the right direction.

> 'A rumour did the rounds at school last year: that if you wash your bits with Coke after sex you won't get pregnant. Well, a few girls ended up getting pregnant, of course. It was the most stupid thing I'd ever heard – and how sticky must that have been, too?'
>
> Binda, 16, Birmingham

Contraception: the ins and outs

There are several different methods of contraception you can use to stop yourself getting pregnant if you have sex, so there's something to suit everyone. For full details of places you can get free contraception and advice, see the 'Further Information' section at the back of this book.

Condoms
Rubber johnnies, willy warmers, love gloves . . . whatever you call them, condoms can be a little

confusing. So, facts first: a condom is a very thin latex sheath which fits snugly over a lad's erect penis. It stops sperm from entering the girl's vagina. This means a condom is a really easy and effective way of preventing pregnancy, and is the only contraceptive (along with the female condom) to stop you getting STIs. You can buy condoms in chemist's and supermarkets, or get them for free at your local family planning clinic or women's health centre.

Female condoms

Yes, they exist – they just don't get much press! This is a polyurethane sheath, which lines the vagina with a flexible ring on each end. The ring on the closed end fits inside your vagina, while the ring at the other end fits over the entrance to your vagina and keeps the sheath in place. They can be a bit fiddly and so aren't very popular, but if used correctly they can protect against STIs and pregnancy. If you're interested in using the female condom you can buy them over the counter in chemist's or get them free along with advice on how to use them at your local family planning clinic or women's health centre.

The contraceptive pill

The 'Pill' is a tablet containing hormones, which the girl swallows. There are many different kinds of contraceptive pill, but the most common type is the combined pill, which contains the hormones oestrogen and progestogen. It stops your ovaries from releasing an egg every month, so there's nothing for the sperm to fertilise.

In most cases you need to take one pill every day for three weeks, then you stop for seven days while you have your period. It's important that you remember to take your pill every day, or it won't work.

If you think this could be the contraceptive for you, make an appointment to see your GP (the doctor at your local surgery) so s/he can assess which contraceptive pill is best for you and give you a prescription. It can seem daunting, especially if you've known your family GP for years, but everything you tell your doctor is strictly confidential. The vast majority of GPs are also very understanding about sexual health matters – after all, they were teenagers once too!

Make sure you read the instruction leaflet that comes with your pills carefully, and ask your GP any questions you have. There are quite a few types of pill and each is slightly different – for example, the level and types of hormones each type of pill contains can vary. They can have some side effects, like nausea or mood swings. The key is to listen to your body and work out which pill works best for you.

If the Pill is taken correctly, it is highly effective at preventing pregnancy. But it doesn't protect against STIs, so for the best protection use the Pill in conjunction with the male condom.

Condoms: a mystery no more

Got questions? Let our super-savvy guide sort them once and for all . . .

THE MYTH: *My lad can't use condoms because he's allergic to them.*

BUSTED: Some lads *are* allergic to latex or spermicide in condoms but you can find polyurethane condoms (like Durex Avanti), or condoms without spermicide, in most big chemist's.

THE MYTH: *Condoms are too expensive.*

BUSTED: They might costs a few pounds in the shops, but you can always get them free at Brook Centres and family planning clinics – see the 'Further Information' section at the back of this book.

THE MYTH: *Putting two condoms on at once means you definitely won't get pregnant.*

BUSTED: Never use two condoms together! The friction from them rubbing together will only make them break.

THE MYTH: *I can wash out a condom and use it again.*

BUSTED: Apart from that being really unhygienic, condoms are only effective for one use as you'll end up tearing holes in it if you try to put it on a second time. As we said before, you can get condoms for free, so use a new one every time.

THE MYTH: *Condoms are a real turn-off.*

BUSTED: You mean getting to grips with sticky rubber doesn't sound sexy? Don't worry – you'll soon find it's no big deal. The best thing is to practise with them a few times before you have sex. That means getting them out of the packet, examining them, practising putting them on your lad or even rolling them out on a banana. You'll feel happier knowing what you're doing and it'll take the pressure off you both when the time comes to have sex. Plus it'll be a huge relief knowing you're protected from STIs and pregnancy!

THE MYTH: *You don't need to put a condom on until you're about to have sex.*

BUSTED: Your lad needs to put a condom on as soon as he has an erection, as the penis can leak pre-come as soon as a lad is turned on.

THE MYTH: *Condoms are too small for my lad.*

BUSTED: Condoms come in a range of sizes, so there will be one to fit him. Trojan does extra-large condoms if he really is too big for standard ones. Any lad who's worth having sex with will want to wear a condom.

THE MYTH: *Carrying condoms is embarrassing.*

BUSTED: Having a condom with you means you're clued up about sex and are prepared to protect yourself.

THE MYTH: *Buying condoms is scary – the person at the till will laugh.*

BUSTED: Do you know how many people buy condoms every day? Thousands. The shop assistant will be too busy planning what to have for dinner to notice what you're buying, so be brave. If it really freaks you out, buy them at a supermarket so you can pick up a magazine, some fruit and a giant bag of popcorn at the same time and spare your blushes.

DO IT NOW! If you're seriously thinking about having sex, sort out your contraception in advance. You'll be so much more relaxed knowing you've got it covered.

Help - the condom's split!

Accidents do happen – so if your condom splits during sex, you realise you've missed a pill or just had unprotected sex, you can get the emergency pill or 'morning after pill'.

Emergency pills can be taken up to three days after sex, and prevent nine out of ten pregnancies if it's taken within twenty-four hours. The longer you leave it, the lower the success rate, so it needs to be taken as quickly as possible.

You can get the emergency pill for free from your GP or a family planning clinic, or if you're over sixteen you can buy it over the counter at pharmacies for around £26.

Sexually Transmitted Infections

There are over twenty-five different STIs, but here's the info on the main players.

Chlamydia

Look out for: This one's tricky – there are few symptoms in women, just a slight discharge or pain sometimes when you pee. But the infection can cause fertility problems later in life, so it's not something you want to go untreated.

If you've got it: If chlamydia's caught early it can be treated with antibiotics, but as with all STIs you need to notify anyone you've slept with so they can get tested and treated too.

Gonorrhoea

Look out for: A yellow or green-tinged watery discharge, pain when you pee, and sometimes itching and an anal discharge. It's caused by bacteria and can also affect your mouth if you have oral sex.

If you've got it: Again, there's a risk it could

damage your fallopian tubes and make it difficult for you to have kids later in life if it's left untreated. You need to stop having sex until you've finished a course of antibiotics.

Herpes

Look out for: Painful cold sore-like spots around your vagina.

If you've got it: Then you've got it for life. Herpes is a virus that stays in your system and can flare up at any time. It's also possible to spread the virus to your mouth if you have oral sex. There are anti-viral antibiotics that can control and reduce the spots, but they aren't a cure.

Syphilis

Look out for: A sore around your vagina or anus.

If you've got it: The initial sore may heal, but the infection can stay in your system for years. It's a serious infection and can affect your reproductive system, heart, skin, bones and brain if left untreated by antibiotics.

None of these STIs are nice to say the least, so the best thing you can do is use a condom to stop yourself from catching them.

And what about HIV?

HIV stands for Human Immunodeficiency Virus and it's mainly transmitted through unprotected sex with someone who's infected. This virus damages your body's ability to defend itself against the infections and diseases that we all come into contact with every day. A person can have HIV for years before it makes them ill, but eventually it leads to AIDS, which stands for Acquired Immune Deficiency Syndrome. This is the point at which people with HIV start to show symptoms of unusual infections; their immune system is really weak and the AIDS infection can cause them very serious illness and death.

At the moment there are treatments for HIV that can slow the progress of the virus, but there's no cure or vaccine. Over 60,000 people in the UK currently live with HIV, and the number is rising. So play it safe, and use a condom.

I think I might have caught an STI . . .

While prevention is better than cure, if you think you might have caught an STI it really is best to get yourself checked out sooner rather than later. Make an appointment to see your GP or look up your local Genito-Urinary Medicine (GUM) clinic –

see 'Further Information' at the back of this book. Some GUM clinics also have walk-in centres where you don't need an appointment. Try not to stress about it – the staff aren't there to judge you and it's totally confidential.

'I'd only been sleeping with my boyfriend Ricky for a few weeks when I noticed it really hurt when I peed. I was too embarrassed to do anything about it at first – I mean, I've known my family doctor since I was a baby. But then I heard I could go to my local family planning clinic to get checked out, which seemed like a good idea.

'I was so nervous when I went along, but the nurse was lovely. She just asked me some questions and took a few swabs. But when the results came back, it turned out I had chlamydia. I was gutted. It must have been from Ricky, ' cause I hadn't slept with anyone else. He had to get tested too.

'We both went on antibiotics and it cleared up after a few weeks. I'm so glad I got checked out though – it could have been nasty if I'd left it. Now Ricky and I use condoms as well as the Pill – just to be on the safe side.'

Gemma, 16, Petersfield

What to do if you fall pregnant

'When I first saw the blue line on my home pregnancy test, I was horrified,' says Katie, 19, from Cardiff. 'I was seventeen, I'd lost my virginity on a one-night stand and, stupidly, we hadn't used a condom. I got pregnant the first time I had sex!'

If you fall pregnant, the most important thing to remember is there are options open to you. You can continue with the pregnancy and keep the baby, or continue with the pregnancy and have the baby adopted. Alternatively, you can have an abortion (a surgical procedure that will end the pregnancy).

Talk to someone

Only you will know which option's right for you and, even if you feel nervous about telling your parents, remember they'll be able to help you decide. 'When I discovered I was pregnant at sixteen, I was too scared to tell mum,' says Nicola, 17, from Nottingham. 'But she knew something was up and asked me directly. She gave me a big hug and said I should have told her sooner. Her support was what helped me cope.'

Your choice

Legally, neither your parents nor the father of the baby can force you into anything. But it's a good idea to talk to them about your options. Even if they're angry at first, most parents come round and want to be there for their daughter. 'It took me two weeks to tell Dad,' says Katie. 'Once he calmed down, he was so kind and even came with me to the doctor.'

Pregnancy isn't something that goes away if you ignore it. You must see a doctor or visit a family planning centre as soon as possible. When you see a doctor or health worker, they'll talk you through your choices and tell you what to do next. Although it isn't a decision to be taken lightly, you have to decide fast. In the UK, abortions are performed up to twenty-four weeks after conception (the day you got pregnant), but the earlier it's carried out, the better.

If it's possible, you should also discuss your options with the boy who got you pregnant, so he knows what's going on. Unfortunately some lads don't want to know, but at least you'll have tried.

Completely confidential

If you decide on an abortion, don't worry about being judged by the hospital staff – you won't be.

Doctors and nurses deal with loads of girls every day who need to terminate an unplanned pregnancy. And, whatever myths you may have heard, abortion doesn't cause infertility. By law, doctors can't tell your parents about the abortion, but you'll need to tell someone, as you'll need the physical and emotional support. Nicola went to the clinic with a mate's older sister. 'She waited at the hospital and took me home afterwards. I wouldn't have got through it without her.'

If a girl's certain she wants an abortion, she'll usually feel relieved when it's over. But you should only go through with it if you're one hundred per cent sure. 'I knew I was doing the right thing because, at sixteen, I wasn't ready to be a mum,' says Nicola. 'And I got to speak to counsellors afterwards, which really helped.'

Whether you decide to keep the baby or not, it's vital you know your options and do what's right for you. After all, you'll have to live with your choice. 'I dropped out of school to have my baby and I don't go out much or see my mates,' says Katie. 'It's very, very tough, but I love my baby and know I made the right choice for me.'

If you need more help or advice on pregnancy, see the 'Further Information' section.

Making yourself happy

There's something that you never seem to hear about in women's magazines, on TV and in books – and that's that sex is meant to be something you enjoy. Often, us girls can get so preoccupied thinking about whether lads find us sexy and whether we're doing things right that we forget that it's meant to be fun for both people. So try to relax, and make sure you explore what's enjoyable for both of you – if that means you have to be a little selfish, so be it!

Exploring your own body and becoming familiar with how it works is an important part of your sexual wellbeing. Stimulating yourself sexually is pleasurable and totally normal. Boys are always joking about masturbation and wanking, but just because girls are more discreet doesn't mean we don't do it too!

First, you need to be somewhere quiet where you won't be disturbed – if you're tense, it's hard to enjoy it. A good place to do this is in the bath or shower, where the heat can really help you relax. The focus of sexual arousal is usually the clitoris – a small, pea-sized lump packed with sensitive nerve-endings, which is tucked under some hood-like folds of flesh at the top of your vaginal lips.

You should find that if you touch or rub on or around your clitoris, it'll produce some pleasant sensations.

Gently play with your clitoris and find what works best for you. Some people find massaging the clitoris in small circular motions with a finger works best. You can also touch other parts of your genitals – the idea is to have fun with it! After a while you may find you can stimulate yourself to orgasm, but don't worry if you can't – masturbation isn't about reaching a goal, it's about learning what makes your feel good.

Your worries: the questions that run through your head

Q. *Is he comparing me to other girls?*

A. If you were in bed with Orlando Bloom, would you be going, 'Well, he's very enthusiastic but just not as bendy as Justin Timberlake'? No – you'd be blooming thrilled he was there with you in the first place, and it's the same situation for lads. Don't forget that boys have as many neuroses about their bodies as we do – Am I too weedy? What if I'm too small? What if I don't last very long? He's going to be too busy worrying about his own stuff to be running a tally on you.

Q. *What if he hates my body?*

A. Unless you've never clapped eyes on each other before (and let's face it, if that's the case – what are you doing jumping into bed together?) he'll already have a pretty good idea of what your figure looks like. Boys are boys: by this stage he's already stared at your bum when you weren't looking, checked out your boobs and has a pretty good idea of your shape. So it's highly unlikely he's going to hate anything about your body at all. Trust us: he's going to be so thrilled you've got your clothes off, you could have six nipples and he wouldn't notice.

Boys answer your hot topic: 'Does it matter how experienced I am?'

'No – you can't judge a girl on stuff like that.'
Mike, 18, Walthamstow

'I don't mind if she's been with loads of other lads, so long as she doesn't go on about it!'
Andrew, 17, Wolverhampton

'If she's less experienced we can learn together.'

Tom, 16, London

'No – it's all about the connection you have, not your history.'

Benji, 19, Glasgow

Burning questions: you ask, we answer

Q. *Last weekend I went to a house party with my friends. I ended up getting off with loads of lads, which was great. But now my mates aren't talking to me, and one of them even called me a slapper. I'm so upset – what did I do wrong?*

A. Your mates are upset because they wanted to have a great night with you, not watch you fling yourself at any guy with an operating tongue! You need to apologise to your mates, and explain that you don't want them to judge you on one night of madness. Try promising them a girls' night out together – without a whiff of a lad to spoil the fun. You might also want to think about why you chose to snog so many guys in one night. Sure, everyone likes to have a good time and it's great to feel attractive, but just because you CAN pull everyone in sight doesn't mean you should. Hold back a little next time – it'll earn you a bit more respect.

Q. *I've being seeing this lad for three months now, and I feel ready to sleep with him. But when I try to take things further, he brushes me off. I'm so confused – I thought all lads want sex?*

A. While all lads might love the idea of having sex, actually doing it can be quite a daunting prospect. Lads are often expected to be rampaging bundles of hormones who'll jump you if you stop talking for two seconds. But many boys are understandably nervous about getting intimate with a girl, especially if it's for the first time. If you're mature enough for sex, you're mature enough to talk about it first. Tell him how you feel, and ask him if he feels he's ready to have sex too. Working through it together will make it a much better experience.

Q. *I want to have sex with my boyfriend, I'm just not ready yet. But my boyfriend says he'll dump me if I don't sleep with him soon. What should I do?*

A. If you're not ready for sex, don't let this lad

pressure you. If he really cares about you, he'll want you to be totally sure and absolutely ready. Tell him exactly how you feel. If he's a keeper, he'll back off – but if he keeps on about it, it's time to ditch him.

Q. *My boyfriend blabbed to his mates about what we did in bed, and now they all keep making jokey remarks. I'm so embarrassed, I could kill him!*

A. What a moron, eh? Unfortunately, some lads do have this huge desire to show off when it comes to sex. He probably knew in the back of his mind that it wasn't the right thing to do, but male bravado tends to take over and they end up boasting about all sorts of stuff. By telling his mates these intimate details, he betrayed you, and you have a right to be upset. He needs to understand that what he did was inappropriate and apologise to you – and it's the least he can do to make his mates shut up with their stupid comments, too.

It's a wrap!

By now you have:

- ⊘ Discovered what you need before you're ready for sex.
- ⊘ Learnt how to say no.
- ⊘ Sussed if he's after love or just sex.
- ⊘ Busted sex myths.
- ⊘ Figured out your contraception choices and understand where to get them from.
- ⊘ Learnt how to take care of your own sexual health.
- ⊘ Know how to make yourself happy.

Going forward make sure you:

- ✪ Stick to your guns – if you say no, you mean no!
- ✪ Are fully prepared if you decide to have sex.
- ✪ Remember the facts about sex and don't fall for the myths.
- ✪ Put yourself first.

CHAPTER 6

Dealbreakers

No relationship is perfect. You start off on a high of excitement, and it's inevitable that the heart-stopping adrenalin rush you get every time you see him begins to wear off as you begin to relax with each other. For many, this can be the best bit. But only you will know if your relationship is making you truly happy. There are some situations where a girl's got to know when to cut her losses and run – and we're not just talking about if he's got terrible taste in trainers.

How do you know if it's just not working out?

Can't think of anything to talk to him about? Dreading your next date? Started spotting dozens of other guys you'd rather be with? These are all signs that you may need to call time on your relationship.

✪ Sit down somewhere quiet and close your eyes. Think in detail about the last three times you saw him, and how you felt. Did you have a laugh together? Did you talk about anything difficult? Were you just plain bored?

✪ Open your eyes and write all the feelings down as quickly as possible:

....

....

....

....

....

....

....

Look at the words you've written above.

✪ Have you written down more negative feelings than positive ones? Are the negative feelings related to things you can talk to him about, or that you might be able to work out together?

✪ Are there loads of positive feelings, over-shadowed by one big negative emotion? Do you feel able to work with him on that one area or problem to make your relationship better?

It's difficult to separate out all the confusing and conflicting feelings you might have about a relationship. By writing things down, then looking back at them, patterns in your subconscious emotions can appear which can help you find your answer.

If there are aspects of your relationship you're unhappy about, but you've got a lot of good stuff in there too, then you need to talk to your lad. Explaining how you feel will either enable you to sort things out or make it clear to you it's not going to work. Either way, an answer is better than hanging about in a relationship that just doesn't make you happy.

Dealbreaker situations

You might find your heart rules your head at times, making it difficult to assess things. If you feel uncomfortable in your relationship but can't put your finger on what it is, try this exercise.

Read through the following scenarios, and mark each one out of ten – one meaning that you honestly feel it's nothing like your relationship, and ten meaning it matches exactly.

Dealbreaker Situation One

Ben is gorgeous and you sometimes can't believe he's going out with you. Trouble is, he never seems to have any money and is always borrowing off you. You don't really mind – you know he'll pay you back at some point. But it's been going on for over a month and he's taking you more and more for granted. The other night you thought you were going to have a romantic night in together, but he said he was off out with his mates and asked if you could lend him a tenner. He can be really sweet, but gets moody if you don't agree to the stuff he asks for. At the back of your mind it's niggling at you, but at the moment you'll forgive him 'cos it's not like he's cheating on you . . .

Mark out of 10: __

Dealbreaker Situation Two

This weekend it's your best mate's birthday. You're desperate for all your friends to meet your new lad, James, but whenever you've tried to organise a get-together in the past he's been less than keen. You put it down to him being too busy or too tired. But this weekend is different. Karen's your best mate in the whole world, and she's having an amazing party in a barn outside town. You spent ages picking out the perfect dress and excitedly chatting about it with your mates. James hasn't said he *can't* make it. But when you double check with him on the Friday, he drops the bombshell: he's not coming, and mumbles something pathetic about meeting the lads in the pub. You can't get him to change his mind.

Mark out of 10: ___

Dealbreaker Situation Three

Jack started off the loveliest guy in the world – bringing you flowers and sending you cute little texts through the day, saying how gorgeous you were. That was what made you fall for him. You loved the way he treated you, it made such a change from the other immature lads you know. But after the first few weeks he began to change. He's stopped calling when he says he will and gets annoyed if you ask him where he's going. You're desperate to have the old Jack back and are hanging on in there, hoping something you do will make him happy and change him back. But the nicer you are, the meaner he gets.

Mark out of 10: ___

Dealbreaker Situation Four

You like Harry because he's a bit older and smarter – he knows what he's doing and is really confident and sure of himself. You wouldn't admit it to anyone, but you're a bit in awe of him, to be honest. Which is what made it so awkward when he started pressuring you to go a bit further than you're comfortable with. He's very persuasive, says you'd do it if you loved him, that you have to do it at some point, so why not with him. You don't want to lose him and feel torn.

Mark out of 10: __

Dealbreaker Situation Five

Steve is affectionate, considerate and loving. Which is why you just can't understand his behaviour. One minute he's telling you you look great, the next he's putting you down in front of your mates. Sometimes he listens to you, others he cuts you off and laughs horribly at you. When you confront him, he says you just can't take criticism or that he didn't mean it. But then he does it again, and each time it hurts. Last week you got really upset with him and threatened to end the relationship, but he got freaked out and said he can't live without you. You love him, but at times you feel trapped.

Mark out of 10: __

Dealbreaker Situation Six

You and Dean used to spend so much time together, he might as well have moved into your bedroom. But over the past few weeks, you've noticed he's been a bit distant. When you ask him what's wrong, he brushes you off and doesn't seem to want to talk about it. He can be hard to get hold of and most nights you have no idea where he is. Once you surprised him when he was whispering on the phone; he looked guilty and hung up quickly.

Mark out of 10: __

Which situation scored highest? Read on to find out what's really happening – and how you should deal with it.

Dealbreaker Situation One: He's using you

This guy just isn't pulling his weight in your relationship. Sure, couples help each other out now and then, but it sounds like he's taking your good nature for granted. If he's on the level, the fact he owes you money will be weighing on his mind, and paying it back to you should be his priority. Next time you see him, tell him you're totally broke and ask if he can pay you back some of the cash he's borrowed. How keen he is to help you out says it all.

Dealbreaker Situation Two: He won't make an effort with your mates

There could be a few reasons he doesn't want to meet your friends – he could be really shy; he could see it as a sign of commitment that he's just not ready for; he could just be lazy. But your friends are a part of you, and he should make the effort. The only way you'll find out his reasons is to ask him. Make it clear that it means a lot to you. If he's shy, arrange for him to meet your mates in small groups at a time. But if he's lazy or lacking commitment to you, he needs a kick up the bum. Give him another month to get his act together, or it's game over.

Dealbreaker Situation Three: He doesn't treat you with respect

Some guys think they only need to be nice in the early stages of going out – once you're hooked, they don't need to make effort any more. This is a sign that he lacks respect for you and your relationship. Every relationship needs constant effort, and once one of you starts taking the other for granted it's only downhill from there. Talk to him about how you feel. Tell him you feel neglected. If he listens and tries to change, he's worth sticking with. If he acts with disdain or ignores your feelings, he needs to be told where to go.

Dealbreaker Situation Four: He's pressuring you into doing stuff you don't want to do

If this lad really loves you, he'd never try to make you do something that makes you unhappy. Lads can be a bit over-eager when it comes to sex, and there's a chance he doesn't realise he's coming on so strong. You need to have stern words with him. A decent lad will be willing to listen and to wait. If he keeps up this behaviour when you've told him quite clearly how you feel, then show him the door.

Dealbreaker Situation Five: He's manipulative

This is one insecure boy, and he's doing a bad job of hiding it. A lad who feels the need to put you down and criticise you only does it for one reason: to make himself feel better. A lad who feels frightened or worthless may secretly believe he's not good enough for you, so he tries to drag you down to his level. He may not realise that's what he's doing, but it's still unacceptable. This kind of behaviour relies on you putting up with it, so don't. Tell him you won't be spoken to like that. And if he doesn't listen? It's time to leave.

Dealbreaker Situation Six: He's cheating on you

Hmm – sounds like your lad is hiding something, and it might be something in a skirt. Everyone has secrets, but when a lad goes from living in your pocket to being cold, uncontactable and guilty-looking, it suggests he's playing away. If he won't talk to you, your only choice is to confront him. Being direct may force him to tell you what's happening – read on for more advice.

The sussed girl's guide to cheating

Unless you catch him in the act or get him to confess, there's no sure way to know your lad is cheating. But tick three or more of these and you might have reason to be suspicious . . .

O He's picking lots of arguments
O He cancels lots of dates
O He's calling less often
O He's paying you less attention
O He's hard to get hold of
O He doesn't like you playing with his mobile

If he cheats on you . . .

Shout or scream at him if it makes you feel better. Keeping it in won't do you any favours.

When you've calmed down a little, let him explain his version of events. He might say something that instantly makes it clear whether it is or isn't going to work out between you, and it'll mean you have fewer questions spinning round your head later.

Then ask him why he did it . . .

If he says it was a stupid mistake, that he's really sorry and won't do it again, there may be some hope of salvaging things. But only if you believe him and are prepared to forgive him.

If he blames you or acts like it doesn't matter, that's a big problem. If he doesn't think cheating on you is serious, then he doesn't have any respect for you and is likely to do it again.

You deserve someone who's faithful and honest. Staying with someone you can't trust will only make you miserable in the long run. So before you make a decision, ask yourself:

✪ Do I believe him?
✪ Can I trust him again?
✪ Can I forgive him?

If the answer to all three is yes, you can work on building your relationship again.

If you cheat on him . . .

Uh-oh – there was a party last night, there was a really hot guy there, you may have accidentally snogged him . . . what now?

No - go to p.159

Has your boyfriend found out yet?

Yes

Did you tell him?

No

Yes

Are you glad he knows?

No

No

Did you tell him 'cos you felt guilty?

Yes

Yes

Sounds like you've secretly been looking for an excuse to break up with him for a while. Apologise to him sincerely, and think about whether this relationship is really what you want.

If this was a one-off, stupid mistake, tell your boyfriend. Explain how it's made you realise how much you care for him, and promise him that you'll never do it again. Fingers crossed!

Do you want to see the guy
you cheated with again?

No   Yes

Is your
boyfriend likely
to find out
about it?

No

Yes

Would you cheat
again if you couldn't
get found out?

No

Yes

You need to tell him
before anyone else does –
it will give you some
integrity. Assure your
boyfriend that it was a
one-off, stupid mistake,
and tell him that hurting
him is the worst feeling
in the world. Then, give
him a bit of space and
hopefully he'll understand.
Good luck!

It sounds like, in your
heart, you don't really
want to be with your
boyfriend at all. Spare
him the pain of hear-
ing about your indis-
cretion and think
about finishing the
relationship before
someone gets hurt.

Telling him might ease your
conscience but it'll leave your boyfriend
feeling awful. Carrying your secret is the price
you have to pay for cheating in the first place
– and in the meantime, think about whether
your boyfriend is really the right guy for you.

It's a wrap!

By now you have:

- ⊘ A clearer idea of how you feel about your relationship.
- ⊘ Worked out if it's time to call it quits.
- ⊘ Sussed which areas of your relationship need more work.
- ⊘ Learnt to spot if he's a cheater.
- ⊘ Discovered how to deal with a cheating situation with minimal pain.

Going forward make sure you:

- ✪ Stay focused about what you will not put up with.
- ✪ Keep putting in effort if you think your relationship is worth saving.
- ✪ Maintain your life balance – you'll always need your friends and family.

CHAPTER 7

The Break Up

From Paris Hilton to Cameron Diaz to Jennifer Aniston, every woman in the world goes through a break-up at some point – and beauty, fame and money don't make any difference. If someone has broken up with you, it can seem like sitting at home listening to the warblings of James Blunt for the rest of your life is your only option. But look on the bright side – at least your break-up isn't documented in minute detail in *Heat* magazine. These things happen – best to get it over with, so you can move on and find the guy who's *really* perfect for you.

The do's and don't's of dumping

It's like waxing your legs – it's not pleasant, but do it fast and it'll hurt less! So that means no dragging it out, no being vague, and no giving him long lingering looks of pity while going 'I . . . um . . .'

DO . . . it face to face
If you went out with him, you must have liked him
– and if you liked him you can at least respect
him enough to tell him in person.

**DON'T . . . leave him a Post-It with 'IT'S OVER!'
stuck to his sleeping mush**
He won't appreciate it – oh, and breaking up by
text, voicemail, and email is out too.

DO. . . go somewhere quiet
It's not really fair if you're in such a noisy place
he has to ask you to repeat that you're breaking
up with him three times. Go somewhere you can
talk in peace.

DON'T . . . tell him in front of his mates
Yes, you know you broke up with him – but if he
wants to tell his mates it was mutual, let him.

DO . . . look sorry
Gleefully waving him goodbye as you head out
for a night on the town with your best mate is
rubbing his nose in it a bit.

DON'T . . . tell him on his birthday
That goes for Christmas, Valentine's Day . . . in
fact any day he may have bought you a present or
might be expecting one.

DO . . . tell him why it's over

Because everyone needs closure. Just avoid making up complicated reasons if the plain fact is that you're just not that into him.

DON'T . . . use the words 'boring', 'wimp' or 'just too small'

Breaking up with him is enough for him to deal with for the day – don't give him a complex into the bargain.

YOUR ACTION PLAN:

Use this space to plan what you're going to say. Remember to keep it as simple as possible, and even if you're upset or angry it'll be easier if you keep it dignified and don't resort to calling him names!

....

....

....

....

....

....

....

'Things hadn't been good between me and Joe for weeks, but I'm a bit of a chicken so I kept putting off the whole "You're dumped" conversation. That didn't stop me moaning to all my mates about how deathly dull he was, though.

'It came back to haunt me one afternoon when I took Joe to a friend's barbecue. When he was introduced to my mate's boyfriend Phil, Phil widened his eyes and said, "Mate, I'm telling you this for your own good – Jess doesn't want to be with you anymore, she says it's like watching paint dry." Joe went bright red and I could have died. I tried to explain, but he wouldn't listen. He still won't speak to me now.'

Jess, 18, Huddersfield

Ten easy ways to end it (but we wouldn't recommend them!)

1. Turn up on a date wearing your mum's wedding dress.

2. Tell his best mate (who'd never do the dirty on him) that it's really him you fancy.

3. 'Girlify' his bedroom with fluffy cushions, pink flowers and his baby photos.

4. Doodle love hearts and 'I luv schnookums' all over his maths book in black marker.

5. Befriend his mum and surprise him by popping round for tea – every night of the week.

6. Ask if he thinks 'baby Britney' will have his eyes or your nose.

7. Gatecrash his five-a-side games and refuse to leave until he's told you he loves you.

8. Pay a fit girl to flirt with him, and then throw a massive strop when you 'catch them together'.

9. Insist on discussing where exactly your relationship's going during all of England's World Cup matches.

10. Choose a quiet moment in class to loudly enquire if he's been to the doctor about his 'personal problem' yet.

All tempting, aren't they? But, seriously, don't do any of them unless you want to be labelled a psycho or a total cow!

DO IT NOW!: Once you've decided to end it, just do it. There's never a good time to do it so it's best to get it over with (exceptions apply – see p.162!).

Cringe!

'Last year, when I realised I didn't want to go out with David any more, I decided the easiest way to end it would be over the phone. So one evening before dinner I rang him up and told him it was over. I did go a bit over the top – I even confessed I'd only gone out with him to get closer to his friend Steve, and finished by telling him I never wanted to see him again! Trouble was, my mum overheard me. She marched me round to his house and made me apologise to him face-to-face for "being mean", while she stood behind me on the doorstep tutting and his whole family listened in from the living room. Yeah, thanks mum!'

Andrea, 14, Bradford

FACT: 31% of you think that breaking up by email is the worst way to end it with someone, while 27% think getting a mate or family member to do it is well out of order . . .

Hana's break-up diary

Thursday 17th May
Saw Tim today. Arranged to meet up on
Saturday to check out that new movie at the
cinema. It's been five months, and I still can't
believe how fit he is. My mates are so jealous!
Wonder if he will ask me to go on hols with him
this summer?

Friday 18th May
Really weird day – I don't know what's going on.
When I walked into the toilets at break, I saw
Lisa and her friend Chantelle whispering about
something. They stopped and stared at me.
Then Chantelle went, 'Hana, you must be
gutted.' 'Gutted about what?' I said. And she
went, 'About Tim seeing that girl from
Islington High. You knew, right?' I just looked
at her. She went all pink, said sorry and ran
out. I've been calling Tim's mobile all day and
left loads of messages, but he's not picking up.
Fiona says I should just ignore Chantelle and
Lisa, that they're stirring. I know she's right,
but I'm really freaked out.

Saturday 19th May
Oh God. Tim came round this morning. He told
me he's been seeing that slapper Ashley from
Islington High for two weeks. Two weeks! He
says it's over between us. I'm never going out
again.

CHAPTER 7: **The Break Up**

Sunday 20th May
Fiona came round today and let me cry on her
new H&M T-shirt for three hours. She brought
a giant bar of Whole Nut. I ate it all.

Monday 21st May
Back at school. Everyone keeps giving me
pitying looks or patting on the shoulder and
saying, 'Forget him, Hana, he's such a loser'. But
it doesn't feel like he's a loser – it feels like I
am. I saw him in the corridor between classes,
and he rushed off the other way. He's still so
cute. Need to cry again.

Friday 25th May
This week has been so hard, but I'm feeling a
bit better. I got really angry last night and
smashed the Killers CD he lent me last month
with my shoe. Mum spent dinner listening to me
listing all the things that are actually really
wrong with him. Like, I hated the way he
chewed his food with his mouth open. Why did
I put up with that for so long? And his feet
smell. Bleurgh. Mum was so sweet, she kept
nodding and agreeing with me.

Monday 28th May
I think it's getting better. I saw him today at
the bus stop and I didn't want to cry or stamp
on his new trainers.

Saturday 2nd June
Major relapse. Bumped into him and Ashley
going round Topshop today. She was holding up
this awful orange dress thing. I can't believe it

- he would never go shopping with me, he said it was boring. What's so good about her? How can he like someone with such terrible taste in dresses, anyway?

Sunday 3rd June
Went out with Fiona and Rachel last night to the club in town. Spent four hours dancing round my handbag. Was totally brilliant – I haven't done that for ages. Very tired today though, need more sleep . . .

Thursday 7th June
Hah! Ashley has dumped Tim! Apparently she says he's 'too immature'. Tim looks like he's swallowed a lemon.

Friday 8th June
I don't believe it. Tim caught up with me as I was walking home from school today. He started saying how pretty I am, and how he'd made this huge mistake, and that he realised he wanted me all along. What a creep! It's made me realise he is a loser. Telling him to get lost was so much fun . . .

Hana, 16, London

FACT: Apparently 23% of you would cut your boyfriend out of all your photos after a break up! Sure, you might be upset now, but instead try to remember the good bits of your relationship and just move on.

The Ex-factor

We've all got 'em – ex-boyfriends. And unfortunately it's a fact that the more you date, the more you get. Whether you're the dumper or the dumpee, here's how to handle those oh-my-God moments with style.

AARGH! You bump into him and his new girlfriend

It happens in slow-mo – you're at a party, the crowds move and there's your ex – with his tongue down the neck of some mini-skirted bird.

Sorted: Whatever you do, don't storm over and drag him off her. Remember that, just because he's poking his tongue down someone else's throat, it doesn't mean he's over you. Boys have meaningless flings in order to heal their broken hearts. So hold your head up, keep smiling and chat to your friends. And remember, some hot new guy is just around the corner!

AARGH! He wants you back

Just received your eighth cuddly toy bearing the words 'I wuv U'? Being woken up in the night by someone warbling Mariah Carey songs under your bedroom window? It's time to kick him into touch.

Sorted: Be firm. Meet him in a public place and tell him that it's over and he has to move on. But be kind – snogging your new fella under his nose isn't the nicest way of getting the message across. Try to keep out of his way to give him time to get over you.

AARGH! You can't get over him

He pulled your best mate, trashed your taste in music and burped the national anthem over lunch. So why can't you get him out of your head?

Sorted: When you spend time with someone you inevitably bond, and it can be hard to get used to them not being there anymore. But if he doesn't want to get back together, you've just got to accept it and move on.

> 'Phil is really good mates with my friend Beth. I didn't think much about it when we got together, but when we broke up it got really awkward. Suddenly I was worried he'd pop up at parties or round at mutual friends' houses. So I talked to him about it. Turns out he felt just as weird about the whole thing. We felt much better after that and now I don't dread bumping into him all the time.'
>
> Marie, 16, Hartlepool

'But he was lovely . . .'
Dealing with a broken heart

Sometimes a break-up can come completely out of
the blue. One minute you're holding hands and
kissing on the swings in the park, the next you're
reeling from his sudden announcement that he
'just doesn't want to be in a relationship'.

When the guy that you think is wonderful dumps
you, it can feel like your heart's been shattered.
You can feel totally rejected and doubts about
yourself can begin to creep in – you wonder what
you did wrong and what was it that put him off.
On top of that, you have to deal with the fact that
your best boy friend has gone, and you really miss
him.

✪ Remember that everyone gets dumped at
   some point. Being dumped doesn't make you
   any less attractive or brilliant – it makes
   you human!
✪ In addition, don't get sucked into believing
   you broke up because of some 'flaw' you have.
   People are more complicated than that – he
   could be a commitment-phobe, or he might
   have issues going on with his friends or at
   home.

✪ You owe it to yourself to be in a relationship with someone who adores you and wants to be with you one hundred per cent. This guy might have seemed like 'The One', but he clearly wasn't. Your guy is still out there.

✪ Every relationship you have, no matter how short, teaches you more about what you want from a lad. If you can learn something from your time together, it'll make your next relationship even better.

✪ Just because you broke up doesn't mean you have to wipe out all your happy memories of being with that person. They might be painful right now, but in a few months you'll be able to think about them with a smile.

If you've broken up with someone you really liked, let yourself feel hurt. Play 'your song' over and over, sniff the T-shirt he once lent you and have a good cry. When you've done that, you're well on the road to feeling a whole lot better – and while you miss him now, the recipe below will help you realise there's more to life than this lad.

A recipe for dealing with being dumped

You will need:

One spangly dress
One pair of stupidly high heels
One MP3 mix of all your favourite dance/rock/pop songs
At least two friends
As much make-up as you can find
DVDs of every girlie film you can think of
Pizzas, chocolate and bananas
One workout DVD and a pair of legwarmers
A large, preferably old, pillow
One big grin

What you need to do:

- ✪ Take the pillow into the garden. Beat the living daylights out of it.
- ✪ Put on a crazy outfit and the legwarmers and do an MTV-style workout in the middle of the living room, full-on posing included.
- ✪ Get your two mates to come round, lugging all of their make-up with them.
- ✪ Spread all the make-up on the floor in front of the TV. Whack on the first of the DVDs, and get experimenting with some new looks.
- ✪ Laugh at each other's clown faces, wipe it all

off and grab some food.

✪ Start again with the make-up. Put on the next DVD.

✪ When you've got a look you love, pull on the heels and the spangly dress.

✪ Dance around your bedroom to the MP3 mix. Singing loudly like an *American Idol* contestant is mandatory.

✪ Eat the banana for energy, slap on the big grin and head out on the town.

Moving on

Write a list of all the reasons you're glad you broke up. It'll help you remind yourself he's not as perfect as you like to believe, and leave you free to focus on all the fun stuff you can do now you're single.

Reasons we broke up:

● ....

● ....

● ....

● ....

● ....

Your newly-single mantra

Think of the freedom! No more watching Arsenal when *Ugly Betty* is on, no more boring conversations about cars, no more having to share your Ben and Jerry's ice cream! To remind you there's more to life than lads and boost your confidence, repeat this three times, twice a day for a month:

'I'm free to do what I want, when I want to.'

You're a young and independent woman, so act like it.

Finally, focus on improving stuff that affects you every day. Write a list of six things you've always wanted to do, but have been too scared, broke or plain lazy to try:

• ....

• ....

• ....

• ....

• ....

• ....

Always wanted to try hip-hop dance classes? Now's a great time to find one and give it a go. Been meaning to make up with a mate you argued with? Bite the bullet and just do it – you've nothing to lose. Want a part-time job to earn money for a shopping spree? Use your initiative and find one. Don't let your fears stand in the way of getting exactly what you want (you'll feel more positive and you might just find your secret hidden hip-hop dancing talent along the way!).

'When Ian said to me out of the blue, "I really don't want to go out with you anymore," I was shocked. He hadn't acted like anything was wrong and I'd only popped round his house to pick up a jumper I'd left there. I spent days crying in my room, listening to crappy love songs. But after a week something snapped. Suddenly I realised he wasn't all that: he was a chicken for running away from our problems – I deserved someone I could rely on. Someone who didn't laugh at my CD collection; someone who told me I looked great more than once in nine months; some-one who reminds me of the bassist from the Arctic Monkeys! I haven't found him yet, but I'm having a lot of fun looking.'

Dee, 17, London

It's a wrap!

By now you have:

- ⊘ Discovered how to make dumping as pain-free as possible.
- ⊘ Figured out how to deal with your ex.
- ⊘ The strength to get over a broken heart.
- ⊘ Learnt how to bounce back from a break-up.

Going forward make sure you:

- ✪ Stay dignified and don't resort to bitching about your ex – he's not worth it.
- ✪ Don't let a break-up stop you dating again (who knows who's round the corner?).
- ✪ Keep busy and have fun!

Just do it!

Now you've worked through all the exercises in this book, you're ready to handle anything lads and love can throw at you. It may be a rollercoaster ride at times, but that's really what makes it so much fun! You're now equipped to reel in any lad, handle the ins and outs of dating with style, communicate with him effectively, and navigate all the highs and lows of relationships with total confidence.

But beyond the practical stuff, you're now also more aware of who you are and what makes you happy, and you have the power to get what you want – and most importantly, the self-belief to go out there and do it. So enough with the hanging around – it's time to show the world what you're made of!

Further information

Contraception, sex and pregnancy

Brook Advisory Centres
www.brook.org.uk
0800 0185 023, open 5 a.m. to 5 p.m, Monday to Friday
– Offers free, confidential sexual health and pregnancy advice and contraception to young people under twenty-five.

The Family Planning Association
www.fpa.org.uk
0845 122 8690, open 9 a.m. to 6 p.m., Monday to Friday
– Offers confidential information on contraception, STIs, pregnancy and sexual wellbeing, and will help you locate your nearest GUM clinic.

Marie Stopes International
www.mariestopes.org.uk
0845 300 8090, open 24/7
– Offers advice and help with contraception, abortion and health screening.

Sexual Health Helpline
www.playingsafely.co.uk
0800 567 123, open 24/7
– Offers confidential advice about any sex concerns.

R U Thinking
www.ruthinking.co.uk
0800 282 930 open 7 a.m. to midnight, 7 days a week
Offers confidential sex advice, facts and answers.

Education for Choice
www.efc.org.uk
– A website designed to help you make an informed choice about pregnancy and abortion.

Sexuality

Gay Youth UK
www.gayyouthuk.org.uk
– A website for lesbian, gay, and bisexual young people and those questioning their sexuality.

The Lesbian & Gay Foundation
www.lgf.org.uk
0845 330 3030 open 6 p.m. to 10 p.m., 7 days a week
– Offers information, help and support.

Domestic Abuse and General Help

The Hideout
www.thehideout.org.uk
- A wesbite for young people affected by domestic violence.

Childline
www.childline.org.uk
0800 1111, open 24/7
- A free helpline for young people where you can talk about any problem to trained counsellors.

Index

www.piccadillypress.co.uk

☆ The latest news on forthcoming books

☆ Chapter previews

☆ Author biographies

☆ Fun quizzes

☆ Reader reviews

☆ Competitions and fab prizes

☆ Book features and cool downloads

☆ And much, much more . . .

Log on and check it out!

Piccadilly Press